Fresh Beginnings

Fresh Beginnings
and other stories

by Leela Dutt
illustrated by Kate Attfield

Bridge House

British Library Cataloguing in Publication Data
A Record of this Publication is available from the British
Library

ISBN 978-1-914199-12-7

This edition published 2022 by Bridge House Publishing
Manchester, England

For lifelong friends who still shape who I am today:
Doris Gardner (1927-2014)
Veronica Hallett (1935-2014)
Vicky Mitra (1942-2016)
Margaret Johnston (1942-2020)

Contents

1. Visitors

It's my father's funeral today. So inside I'm a jelly. But outside – pure steel.

Meanwhile, way out in the so-called real world, up to a billion people are said to be glued to their television screens waiting for a couple of American guys to step onto the dusty surface of the moon for the first time without a care in the solar system.

But none of that has anything to do with me, because I've just lost the best friend I ever had: Evan Griffiths, born Carmarthen 1910, resident of North London. He died last week at the Edgware General of complications following surgery for cancer, ridiculously young – not even a pensioner. So I am not in the least interested in the first moon walk today; they say there will be plenty more of them in the future.

I've reached Golders Green crematorium an hour early, and there's only one other person outside, an elderly woman.

"Hi there, Jennifer! I thought some extra flowers might come in useful…" She looks at me with a kindly smile.

Damn! We haven't done flowers. My mother said you couldn't be expected to deal with anyone as trivial as a florist, for God's sake, at a time like this.

"I can get some more if you like," the woman goes on.

Can't quite place her for the moment. She's clutching a massive armful of summer blooms in brilliant colours. "Sorry it's too late for his favourite daffodils!"

Ah, she knows Dad, then. She looks familiar – grey hair with tinges of red, probably a member of the family on Dad's side. Not sure who – reminds me of great-aunt Morag – who died when I was little.

"Oh, that's really kind of you, er…?"

"Call me Jay – everyone does, these days." She sticks her hand out and her grasp is firm.

Dad's is the first cremation of the day, so they let us in early. *Help! I'm going to start sneezing* – there's an ancient dusty smell in here. It's a huge place, this chapel, and Jay's flowers don't go far. She whips out a little black thing from her pocket and taps a few buttons on it, then she presses it to her ear. *Oh, gosh, has she got earache?*

"Hi, it's me," she says, gazing up at the ceiling. "Yes, I'm here at the crem… Fine… Signal's OK so far. Listen, Kate, can you bring five or six more bunches of flowers when you come? Thanks… I'll see you soon – got to go!"

9

Then she puts the little black thing back in her pocket; *what the hell is it?*

"My daughter will sort something out." Apparently she's talking to me again. "You're looking great, by the way, Jennifer; turquoise really suits you. And your hair is just right."

Which is not at all what my mother said this morning; she told me it was a pity I could never do anything with my hair these days. Mother went on to inform me that it didn't really matter, since I only work with primary school children. But the turquoise was her idea – Mother comes from Holland, and she maintains that the obsession over here with black for funerals is ridiculous.

"And how's the writing going?" says Jay.

What? How the hell does she know about that? No one knows that I write. No one at all – well except for Duncan of course, but that doesn't count; sometimes I think Duncan lives inside my head. Oh, and I told my sister Sue once, but she wasn't listening.

There's a noise at the back, and several more people have arrived.

Oh, good heavens! There's Duncan after all; I didn't think he'd get time off work to come. *How very kind of him!* He's the father of Joey in Standard Two, the class I teach. He's also an old friend of Dad's; they met at bookbinding classes, of all things, at the institute where I went to school. He lives alone with Joey now, since his wife died a couple of years ago. I've got a lot of time for Duncan.

"Morning, Jennifer." Duncan is coming over, his thick black hair flopping untidily over his eyes. "How are you feeling?" He looks at me solemnly and shakes my hand – I don't think we've ever shaken hands before. It feels good. "Today must be a big ordeal for you, but you look stunning. You always do." I grow six inches and the jelly inside begins to set.

Why is everyone suddenly telling me... Oh look, my sister Sue's just sailed in. She's positively blooming, carrying all before her, in a tasteful black maternity dress. She's not actually due for another six weeks, but you wouldn't think she could get much bigger. Drippy Tim is following in her wake as usual.

"Is Mother here yet?" Sue calls out. "We ought to wait outside till she comes, don't you think?"

Duly we all troop outside and stand gazing up at the huge plane trees lining Hoop Lane. I know this road so well – I walked up here every day for eleven years when I was a child. When I was very small Dad used to walk with me.

Jay disappears for several minutes and comes back with some more flowers – *where has she got them from?* But there's no time to think about that. I glance at my watch after twenty minutes – time is passing – and Mother is cutting it fine. *Presumably she is planning to turn up?*

"Tim has only just managed to fit the funeral in," Sue mutters as we stand waiting. "He's off to Edinburgh to see his supervisor tonight." She pauses to wipe what looks like an egg stain from Tim's black tie.

At last the car bringing Mother comes round the corner, followed by the hearse, and we all turn towards it.

My brother Max leaps out of the car first, and dashes round to open the door for Mother. She glances up, taking in what is quite a crowd by now, and regally stretching out her legs she steps onto the pavement, taking Max's arm for support. She smells strongly of *Eau de Cologne*.

"Thank you, all of you, for coming, thank you so much," she murmurs. Effortlessly she has become the focus of all attention.

No change there, then.

The coffin is unloaded and wheeled into the chapel in front of us. Oh, how small it is! Dad isn't – wasn't – a big

11

man, but he was big to me, not only when I climbed onto his knee as a young child, but later as I grew up and took him for granted, my rock that would always be there. Now he is reduced to that tiny wooden box those men are wheeling in. *No, stop. This is all wrong!*

Glancing over my shoulder, I catch Duncan's eye. *Oh God, he must be thinking of the day of his wife's funeral!* Poor Duncan, and how very brave of him to come today in spite of that. He gives me a faint flicker of a smile, and I try to smile back. *What a dear person he is!*

Max leads Mother slowly towards the chapel, and the rest of us follow, Sue and I tucking in behind them. I've given the sign for the organist to begin, and she plays some rather fine Bach, one of Dad's favourites. She's a very good musician.

"Oh, I love this piece!" cries Jay, falling into step beside me. "I got a CD of it from Amazon last year."

I have no idea what the woman is on about, or indeed what Brazil has got to do with anything, but I let it pass over my head.

As we shuffle into place in the front row, Mother erupts into a sudden burst of hysterical sobbing. The minister allows a decent interval before he begins proceedings.

Jay has slipped in next to me in the front row, which is meant to be reserved for close family only, but I guess it doesn't matter. Mother stops sobbing abruptly and gives her a hard stare, but Jay just nods at her and smiles benignly.

As the minister begins to speak, Jay takes out the mysterious black thing from her pocket and points it at Dad's coffin. She looks intently at it for a moment and then presses a button. I must ask her later what she's up to, if there's time.

After a while they put on one of Dad's favourite records – a male voice choir from the Welsh valleys. He used to play it a lot – when he was fed up with life in London – or perhaps with Mother. He'd go upstairs on his own to a little room we called his cubbyhole and play them.

Guide me, O thou great Jehovah...

I've got a horrible feeling I'm going to cry. Not out loud like Mother, of course; I never do that. But tears are beginning to stream down my face.

Feed me till I want no more... Dad used to say that was what a line of rugby forwards shout when they pass the ball along. I think he was joking! He was deeply into rugby; he used to take me to Twickenham to watch Wales.

I'm not the only one crying; Jay is too, at least as much as I am, she must have known Dad really well then; *so how come I don't recognise her?*

Even my brother Max is surreptitiously wiping away the odd tear from his eyes. He likes to pretend he's big and hard, does Max.

Things are dragging on a bit now, and Mother is drumming her fingers on the front of the pew, not quietly. She's looking pointedly at her watch, and she taps it to see if it is still going. *Oh God this is so rude* – I just hope the nice minister doesn't notice.

He has, and he's looking straight at Mother. *What are the chances of a big hole opening up in front of me and swallowing me up? Not great.* I used to pray for that when I was a child and Mother was being particularly embarrassing in a shop or a bus queue, but God never saw fit to oblige.

Saved! The organist strikes up again, and at last it is time for the coffin to slide away behind the curtain.

Is that it, then? Goodbye, Dad!

We all stand up, and Max leads Mother down the aisle, followed by the rest of us. Duncan catches my eye and smiles.

13

My sister stumbles as she gets to the back, and I grab her arm swiftly. "You OK, Sue?"

"Course I am – don't fuss, Jennifer!" But I don't like the way she's clutching her bulge as though she thinks it's going to escape.

Mother has insisted that everyone should come back to the house after this, and I jolly well hope a fair number of them do, because I have arranged catering for a moderately sized battalion or two and I don't want it wasted.

We sort ourselves out into cars – Max with Mother of course – and I squeeze in with Sue and Drippy Tim. Jay isn't with us anymore – she's cadged a lift off Duncan of all people. She's got a young woman with her now, another person I don't recognise – but oddly she reminds me a bit of Duncan: she has his huge brown eyes, dark floppy hair, although her prominent nose reminds me of Dad. She looks friendly. Jay goes off muttering something about her carbon footprint, whatever that is. I don't suppose Duncan was even intending to come back to the house, but he's got to now he's agreed to bring them.

As I look properly at my sister, I can see she is quite exhausted, and when I press her she admits she hasn't been sleeping well for some time.

Ah good – the caterers are already here and they've got everything set out – as promised. It all looks very clean and nice, with white tablecloths on trestle tables, some in the house and some in the garden, and there's an appetising smell of sausages and coffee. Mother decides to stand by the front door greeting guests as they arrive, while I tell people where the loos are. I recognise nearly everyone; a few cousins down from Wales that I haven't seen in a while, and a lot of Dad's colleagues from the office. I'd better talk to them and offer them some bridge rolls.

"What have you got here?" I turn round as Mother's

voice rings out in the hall. She is confronting a waitress who looks about fourteen, in a black and white uniform.

"Er... egg and cress, madam," the child mutters. "I think."

Mother lifts up the edge of one of the bridge rolls, and the plate wobbles in the girl's hand. "Oh no, that won't do. Won't do at all. Egg, you say? All I can see is a thin scraping of something white... Pathetic. Where's the smoked salmon?"

"I don't know..." the poor girl stammers. "I don't think there is any. Or maybe in the other room..."

Jay rushes up at once. "Oh, come now, Mrs Griffiths! That's not the way to speak to the young lady, is it?"

Mother stares at her.

"These people have all worked their butts off to provide a feast for you and your guests, and the least you can do is treat them with courtesy," Jay says, with a reassuring smile at the waitress, which seems to include Mother. "I'll have an egg and cress one – ooooh, my favourite! Thank you so much, dear; you're doing a great job. Now come along with me, Mrs G, and we'll see if there is any smoked salmon. I rather fancy there may be..."

Jay puts her arm around my poor, astonished mother's shoulders and steers her firmly into the sitting room. There's a look of what I can only call deep satisfaction on Jay's face.

"Close your mouth, Jennifer – something might fly into it!" Duncan appears behind me, laughing, and I join in.

I think everyone's got something to eat by now. What about the drinks? Is there enough sherry?

"Stop worrying, Jennifer!" Duncan is still beside me – actually he's been a great help, directing people to the different tables in the garden, finding seats for the older visitors and fetching them drinks. He's good with old ladies, I've discovered. "Everyone's OK. Relax!"

There's a sudden burst of laughter from the group next to us, and we turn to look. *Sounds as if they are talking about this wretched moonwalk.*

"When are they going to land, do you know?" someone says.

"Should be today – I can't wait to see it!"

"No, nor me!"

"So dangerous – what if they miss?"

"Are they actually going to get out of their space craft and walk on the ground? I can't imagine it!"

"Ah yes…" I notice Jay in the middle of this group. "That's one small step for man, a giant leap for mankind."

There is an astonished silence.

"Wow!"

"What did you say?"

"Hey, that's rather good," says Duncan. "Did you just make that up, Jay?"

She blushes and laughs. "No, no. I must have read it somewhere. In fact, it ought to be one small step for *a* man, not man – to get the contrast with mankind – you see? But transmission is difficult, and anyway Neil Armstrong is overcome with awe, obviously."

"Who's Neil Armstrong?" someone asks.

I've no idea, either, but I think I've heard the name recently.

Mother has adjourned to the garden – how lucky we've been with the weather! She's sitting on the bench, holding forth, and several guests relax on deckchairs around her. Dad's roses are looking splendid and are much admired. I love the smell of our garden in the summer. Max mowed the lawn yesterday, and it freshly mingles with the flowers.

You ought to be here showing the place off, Dad – why aren't you?

16

"Your father was very proud of his garden, wasn't he?" Duncan looks at me solemnly. "And it will live on, you know. Hang onto that, Jennifer."

At the back of the garden, under the apple tree, the young woman who appeared with Jay is standing still and pointing something at the crowd. My brother Max is talking to her.

"Who is that – do you know, Duncan? She came in your car, didn't she? I've never seen her before."

"Nice young woman – she's Jay's daughter, apparently. She's called Kate."

"Look, she's got one of those tiny things that Jay had – what on earth is it?"

"No idea. Let's go and ask her."

We make our way over, threading through the crowd.

"Kate has just been showing me," Max says excitedly. "Look, it's a camera!"

A camera? I don't see how that would work. It's far too small and flat, for one thing.

"I'm going to transfer these pictures to my laptop and email them to everyone," Kate explains.

"You're going to what…?" Duncan asks.

"My big brother Joey wants to put them in his blog."

His what?

She flicks a few buttons on it and the most amazing pictures appear on a little screen: there's Mother sitting on the garden bench, and then – another button – we make out a picture of the whole of the back of our house, looking rather fine, framed by trees on either side. *You should see this, Dad!*

"I must take one of you two," Kate declares. Obviously she means me and my brother, but no – she seems to be looking straight at Duncan and me. *Us? No one has ever photographed us together before.* He puts his arm around

17

my waist, which is rather a pleasant sensation I have to say, and he smiles into the little gadget Kate is holding up. She steps back and clicks several times.

There is a sudden commotion behind us as Mother lets out a great moan. "Oh, what is going to become of me, without my wonderful Evan!" An auntie pats her shoulder sympathetically.

"At least you've got your children," says someone on a deckchair. I think they are trying to be helpful.

"Oh, but they have got their own lives – they won't want to bother with little me!"

Little?

"My son is frightfully clever, you know. And ambitious, of course. And my daughter is having a baby in a few weeks – she is totally wrapped up in that. She and her husband, they both are. Can't talk about anything else."

Some sympathetic nodding goes on. "Only natural, isn't it?" someone says.

"But at least there's Jennifer. She does have a job, but she's only a primary school teacher. She will be leaving her flat and coming back to live with me now that Evan is gone. I think that would be the best thing. It will save her money – she can hardly afford her flat, and you should see it – it's tiny! She'll be glad to give it up."

Jay sits up. "Oh, now come on, Mrs Griffiths – you don't mean that, do you? Jennifer needs her independence just as much as Max and Susan do. She's got her own plans for life…"

"But I wouldn't interfere! I never interfere with any of my children…" says Mother, flustered.

That is a matter of opinion.

"Ah but you do, you know! Mrs G, you have never been shy of putting forward your own views on everyone else's lives, have you?"

18

Mother considers this. "Well, I'm certainly not one of those wishy-washy English women who can never pass a judgment on anything!"

Jay laughs. "No, indeed you're not!" She puts her hand lightly on Mother's arm. "But you see, you don't always allow other people to breathe. To think for themselves. You are convinced you know the best for people. You have to step back a bit. Try not to suck the life out of them."

Mother glares at her, speechless for once. *It's not like Mother to take this lying down; what is going on?*

"Look, it'll be alright – believe me, Mrs Griffiths," says Jay. "You have far more inner strength than you realise…"

People are starting to leave at last, and Duncan is fetching coats. But I haven't seen my sister for some time, and Drippy Tim is looking for her anxiously.

"She went upstairs to the loo," he tells me. "But that was ages ago."

"Don't worry, Tim – I'll go and check," I say.

I run into Jay at the top of the stairs.

"Ah, there you are, Jennifer – Susan needs to get to hospital. Now!"

"What? Why? She's not due for six weeks…" I am confused.

She smiles. "They have their own ideas of when they are ready to come, these babies! Her waters have just broken. She needs to get there quite soon. Can you find Tim? Best if we call them a taxi. You can take care of their car, if they leave it here, can't you?"

I'm struggling to take all of this in.

"Oh, and Jennifer…" she adds as I turn to go downstairs. "Don't keep calling him Drippy Tim! He's got hidden depths, I tell you. He's not at all drippy – as you will surely find out!"

Look I know I've always thought of him as Drippy Tim,

ever since my poor gullible sister married him, but I have never ever uttered that phrase out loud. I swear I haven't. Is she reading my thoughts, or what?

After that, everything is confused. Non-Drippy Tim phones for a taxi and hands his car keys over to me. Mother has the situation explained to her and decides that it isn't worth her while to panic because no one would take any notice. My sister comes downstairs, looking pale but somehow radiant at the same time; I've never seen her like this before. I am quite envious.

They're off! We watch the taxi sweep down the road and turn the corner out of sight.

"They'll be OK, don't worry, Jennifer!" Jay is standing by my side in the street. "And before the end of the day you'll be the auntie of a fine..." She hesitates. "Let's just say, a beautiful baby."

Oh my goodness. I guess she's right. I'm going to be an auntie!

"And as for Duncan..." Jay goes on.

"What about him?"

"Nothing... Just, I suppose you do realise he's in love with you?"

I stare at her.

I don't know what to say.

"Maybe I shouldn't have said that," Jay adds. "But I think you knew anyway, didn't you, Jennifer?"

I take a deep breath.

"And now Kate and I must be off too," says Jay briskly. "Where's she got to?"

"Will I see you again?"

She looks at me silently for a moment. "I don't know, Jennifer. Maybe. But probably not."

Kate comes rushing up at that point. "Mum, are you sure we mustn't tell them to bet on Obama?"

Who?

"No, we've been through all this, Kate. You know perfectly well it wouldn't work!"

Kate shrugs her shoulders.

"Have you come a long way?" I ask them.

She smiles. "Yes, you could say that."

On a sudden impulse I lean forwards and plant a kiss on her cheek.

She smiles and grips my shoulders. "Take care, Jennifer!"

"Oh, have they gone already? What a pity, I wanted to say goodbye..." Duncan has been busy tidying up the chairs in the back garden. "Interesting woman, that Jay. I'd like to have talked to her more. How did you say she's related to you, exactly?"

"I'm not sure, to be honest. She felt very close, somehow. But I've never seen her before in my life, as far as I can remember."

He looks at me. "Yes, that's exactly how I felt! She was very close, but I've no idea why."

Then he smiles and touches my arm lightly. "Jennifer... You've done incredibly well, today. You must have been dreading it."

Now he's reading my mind too, the way Jay's been doing all day! Weird.

"Would you... I wonder, would you let me take you out for a meal? Soon?"

"Oh! Well yes... That would be nice. Thank you, Duncan."

He gives me a great, big grin now, and takes my hand in his as we turn and walk back to the house.

2. The Ocarina

A thunderous bang, broken glass splintering in my lap –
who the hell put that Ford Escort in front of me?

I opened the door warily and stepped onto the slipway of
the A470 – and into a stream of oily, grey liquid gushing out
from what had until recently been my aunt's radiator. This was
my first introduction to Wales, over a quarter of a century ago.

"Are you alright?" A woman was running towards me
from the Escort – middle-aged, roughly my height, pleasant
curly hair, wearing jeans and an anorak.

"I'm so sorry," I said. "I just didn't notice that you'd
stopped. I was looking over my shoulder for a gap in the
traffic…"

I guess I wasn't supposed to admit responsibility.
Presumably Aunt Ikuko's insurance would be up to date –
but what on earth was I going to tell her when she got back
from her vacation in Japan?

The woman introduced herself as Meg Davies. "Don't
worry, I'm pretty sure I can still drive *my* car." She shot me
a perceptive glance. "You'd better come with me, son – you
can ring a garage from my home. I only live five minutes
from here, over in Tongwynlais. But we ought to push your
car out of the way first…"

Fifteen minutes later Meg had made me a large mug of

hot, sweet tea and sat me at the table in her snug kitchen. "Just what the Guides taught me to do with shock," she laughed, and I must admit it was welcome. "You on your holidays, then, Takao?"

I explained that my uncle is a manager at the Sony factory in Bridgend. After six years as an engineering student in the States, I'd come over to see if I wanted to work with him in Wales for a time.

"Oh my goodness," she said. "What a terrible thing to happen to you on your first day here!"

The back door opened and in walked a young woman who was taking off a motorcycle helmet and shaking loose her long, sandy hair.

"What's up, Mum? You had a bump, then?" She turned and saw me at the table. "Oh, hiya. All righ'?"

She looked slightly startled when I stood up and bowed at her.

"This is my daughter Rachel – she's another engineering student – like you, she's at Swansea Uni."

Meg explained what had happened.

"What sort of insurance have you got?" Rachel asked me at once. "Me, I've only got third party – can't afford comprehensive. Not worth it for my old bike, but…"

For the past half hour there'd been a nasty thought lurking at the back of my mind; now it swam reluctantly to the surface. "My uncle drives a brand-new Honda," I told them. "No way would he let me touch that! But this is just my aunt's old runabout – I'm almost certain it's third party only. Oh, don't worry, Mrs Davies – it will cover *your* car."

Rachel turned to her mother. "Tell you what, Mum – we'll have to get Grampy to have a look at Takao's car. He's a wizard with cars is my Gramps." She smiled at me. "When he's feeling well. Used to run a repair garage before he retired."

But Meg hesitated.

"Shall I ring him, Mum? My boyfriend Simon could give you a tow up to Grampy's house in Porth if you like," she said to me. "Simes drives a pick-up truck for work."

"No," Meg said sharply. "No, best let me phone Grampy."

Rachel was surprised.

"He can be a bit funny, your grandfather. He was a prisoner during the war, see – he worked on the Burma railway." She seemed to assume I would know all about that.

As Meg left the room, Rachel sat down and passed me the packet of chocolate biscuits.

"Will your father be angry about your Ford?" I asked, tucking in.

She looked blank. "Oh! No, I haven't got a father – he cleared off when I was about two. My brother doesn't even remember him. Don't worry – Mum won't mind you smashing her Escort so long as it gets mended quickly so she can get to her precious choir."

"In a church?"

"No, we don't go to church! Mum's in this Red Choir. They sing all these revolutionary songs. They're good, mind. And nice and loud, like."

Meg came back into the kitchen. "It's alright, Takao. My father says he'll have a look at it if Simon can tow it up to Porth tonight."

"Is Gramps better, Mum? You said he was bad again last week."

"Oh yes, he swears he's fine." Meg turned to me. "My father has angina but try getting him to rest...! He's expecting us at about seven."

When I remember the journey we made up to Porth that evening, words like "contra-flow", "roundabout", "towrope" and "nightmare" spring readily to mind. Luckily Meg offered to sit next to me in Aunt Ikuko's poor little car after we had retrieved it from the slipway and fastened it securely to Simon's truck. I think she was worried about her father's reaction to me.

Simon turned out to be a well-built cheerful young man in a grubby white cap advertising the National Lottery. He'd clicked his tongue sympathetically when he saw the Micra's stove-in front, and offered his opinion that if anyone could deal with that, Rachel's Grampy was the man. "Old Ted Roberts has been mending cars for sixty years," he said.

"There's always a lot of traffic in Ponty," Meg warned me. "Watch out, Takao – he's going to turn right at the next lights – it's the new one-way system."

The driver in the red Ferrari next to us turned and glared at me as I swung dangerously round, the Micra barely under my control.

Porth was an endless sequence of steep narrow streets of terraced houses, most of which Simon was apparently obliged to drive up. When we finally came to rest in an alleyway running along the back of Grampy's road, I put the brake on and took a deep breath.

"You'll need a new radiator of course," Mr Roberts said some half an hour later. "A mate of mine can get one cheap. It's not as bad as it looks, the damage, like. Shouldn't cost you too much." He showed me in some detail what was wrong.

He was a slightly-built, short man – shorter than me. His hair was white. I had the impression that he hadn't shaved for a day or two, and his eyes were slightly bloodshot. I gathered he was a widower living alone, but with Meg's brother's large family living in the next street. He'd nodded briefly at me when we all arrived, making no

25

comment when his daughter introduced me. I felt that he didn't want to talk to me more than courtesy demanded, but when it came to showing me how he proposed to mend the Micra, then his eyes lit up in spite of himself.

"Come back after the weekend," he said, "and I'll sort something out. I likes a challenge. Can't promise anything, mind…"

As I thanked him profusely, Meg declared that they had not eaten yet and she was sending Rachel down the chippie straight away. "We're going to make sure you have something with us this time, Dad. I know what you're like when you're on your own!"

The old man's living room was so small and crowded with furniture that it reminded me of my own family home. I squeezed in next to Simon on the sofa, newspaper balanced on our laps, sprinkling extra vinegar onto my cod. As I looked around the room, I noticed several photographs: an ancient sepia wedding picture of Meg's parents, a recent portrait of one of her nieces getting her degree – and there, tucked away behind a vase of flowers, I saw a faded, grey photo of a dozen soldiers in tropical gear, grinning out from under a palm tree. Mr Roberts noticed me examining it, and I looked away swiftly.

I caught the train up to Porth the following week.

"I've done my best with this, Takao. I took it up to my workshop. Well, I say mine, but of course I had to sell out years ago. My old partners still let me use it. We've put in a new bonnet – here, have a look for yourself, then we'll take her out for a test run."

Lovingly he opened it up. I was impressed, and asked him how much I owed. Most of the parts he'd been able to get from a scrap yard, apparently. He quoted a price which sounded absurdly cheap to me, and I said so.

"To be honest with you, I've enjoyed doing it. It's a long time since…" The old man gave me a sharp look. "Have you got time to come in for a cup of tea? I've got something I want to show you."

I agreed at once. In the living room he went straight to the top drawer of the chest and took out a battered cardboard shoebox. I could tell from the string around the bundle of letters and faded photographs it had not been disturbed for many years. There, tucked away under them was a little round hollow object with a stem and four holes in the front. I guessed it was some kind of whistle, and indeed the old man gave it a brief rub, took a deep breath and then, putting the stem in his mouth and arranging his fingers over the holes, he began to play a slow, lingering folksong on it. It was beautiful.

"Know what this is? It's an ocarina."

"Yes?"

"It belonged to a mate of mine. An Australian. Josh taught me to play it; we shared a hut – us and a couple of dozen other prisoners. Meg told you I was on the Burma Railway?"

I nodded. "I'm afraid I know very little about that period."

"That's a pity. They should teach you, you kids. After all, they're always going on to the German youngsters about Belsen an' that. You weren't born then. I suppose your *parents* weren't even born?"

"No."

He was silent for a moment.

"They weren't all bad. The guards. There was this one chap I remember – very young, he was. Looked a bit like you. You suddenly reminded me of him, last week when Meg brought you here."

"Did I really?"

"He was terrified of the officers above him, mind. Used to skulk around our hut... That's how he heard Josh teach me to play this little thing. It was Josh that saved my life, you know."

"Yes?"

"He was a doctor, see. Back in Melbourne. So he knew which of the local grasses it was safe to eat. Many of the other lads died of starvation – thousands of them – but Josh would pick out the shoots that weren't poisonous, growing on the edge of the camp, and get us to eat them."

"What happened to Josh?" I asked after a pause.

"Oh, he got into some sort of trouble – I forget what. He was taken off for punishment. When he – died – this young guard who looked like you, like, he had to search Josh's things. He came up to me next day with this ocarina in his hands and gave a quaint little bow – just like you did yourself – when you came last week! And he asked me if I wanted to keep it, to remember my friend by. I haven't played it in years."

I took it from him and turned it over gently in my hand. "I don't suppose... Could you show me how to play it?"

He gave a slow smile. "I could have a go."

A couple of hours later we took the Micra up the valley to Treorchy and then, because Mr Roberts wanted to see how it would cope with a good, steep hill, we went up over the Bwch. The view across the open mountainside was marvellous, and the tune Ted had taught me to play echoed in my head all the way.

"She handles alright, don't she?" he said.

"Oh yes! My aunt won't know the difference." I was delighted.

"She'll know it's been sprayed. It's always difficult matching the colour. Meg says the insurance have sorted out her car so she's happy."

That was a relief, I can tell you.

"She says she's going to invite you to one of her Red Choir concerts," he went on with a grin. "Something big at the end of the month – now what did she say it was for? Palestine, I think it was."

I told him I enjoy a good choir.

"Well you can go, then. She wanted me to go too of course, but I told her I couldn't be bothered going down to Cardiff on my own just for that."

"Oh, but now you've mended my car, I could pick you up," I said, "if you like."

He turned to me. "You serious, boy?"

"Certainly. You could give me another lesson on your ocarina – would you?"

The concert was fantastic. I didn't know the music, but it seemed to come from all over the world. South African songs of protest, Latin American sugar planters' ballads, and lots more. Meg was there in the front row, wearing a bright red jersey like the rest. Ted listened intently to the singing, his face bright and sparkling, and he stood up to clap.

"Thanks, Takao," Meg said to me in the interval.

"Whatever for?"

"For bringing my dad down for the concert. I can't remember when I last saw him enjoy himself so much!"

As I drove him back to Porth afterwards, I asked Ted if he had ever sung in choirs himself. Apparently he had sung a lot when he was younger, and enjoyed it.

"Why don't you sing anymore?" I asked. "You've got time now, surely?"

He looked at me. "Time, yes. Plenty of time, Takao. But no more puff! Can't get my breath properly now, see..."

I didn't know what to say to that, and I drove in silence up the A470.

29

Ted had a fatal heart attack that night.

"He probably didn't even wake up," Meg told me the next day. "Oh no, don't you start crying, Takao – you'll set me off again! But there was just one thing: he seems to have written you a note last night. We found an envelope by his bed with your name on it and a small lump inside it – I can't think what it is."

"Oh!" I opened it and took out the ocarina. The scrap of paper simply read, *Thought you might care to have this to remember me.*

The Ocarina was first published in *Kingfisher Blue*, a single-author collection by Leela Dutt, 1996

3. A Touch of Natural History

Brad squirts the hose straight up into my mouth, full force, and the glorious water splashes my face and down my chest, tickling me over and over. Wonderful! Just what I wanted... The smell's good too. Not that this clean, antiseptic water has much of a smell, but it reminds me of ancestral pools with the tang of jungle and heat and some tasty insect larvae to eat.

"Cut that right out, Brad!" Mr Mackenzie is always the one to control things, stop the fun.

I stretch my arms and legs out, begging Brad to continue.

But wait – the lads have got someone new here today.

It's a female, clearly. A young one, no older than Brad, with a lithe body that she's poured into some fetching black jeans and a tight-fitting, black tee-shirt. She's got long, curly, blonde hair, and they are calling her Laurel – what a pretty name – Brad has lost no time pointing out. She claims she's a zoology major.

"He loves it – he always points to 'water' on the lexigram," Brad protests.

"That's so cute." Laurel smiles engagingly at me, and all at once I feel warm all over. "I need to take some photos for my project – I'll just get my camera."

"Hey, you realise they are our closest living relatives, Laurel?" Brad goes on. "So I guess you'd like a bit of water too, wouldn't you?"

And abruptly he turns away from me and squirts the hose at the girl's face instead. *Not fair, my turn! My turn!*

"Bradley, what the heck are you doing?" The boss erupts with fury, his face red, his eyes blazing.

Would you believe, the young lady seems to like it! She's howling with laughter, bending over as the jet of water splashes her face and runs all over her tee-shirt and jeans. Her hair is getting soaked too, and her curls hang in straggles down her face, making her look wild and enticing, Brad seems to think.

But Mr Mackenzie is still furious, the veins standing out on his neck. They are weird, these creatures; I don't know why Laurel doesn't just defuse the situation by taking the incandescent man off for a quickie, as my own folk would do. But these guys are too repressed for that; wearing clothes must be a drawback.

Next morning Laurel is still here – that's good. She's dried her jeans and found another top, this time a crisp white cotton blouse with three-quarter length sleeves. She's got a lovely scent about her today.

There are more visitors, a boy and a girl who have come because there's no-one else to look after them. Old Mackenzie is filling them up with boring facts about where my family came from in the Congo and how we know how to climb a tree and make a bed out of the branches, but they aren't a bit interested in all that – they just want to play with my lexigram.

"Where's the banana?" the boy asks me, and they fall about with amazement when I point to the right picture. You know what, it works every time. *Heck, it's not rocket science.*

"So where are the peanuts?" the little girl asks me. *That's a no-brainer – they are in the top row. Obviously. Anyone can see that. But let's put some new ideas into their heads* – I point at "strawberries" and "blueberries" but sadly no one takes the hint. Marshmallows are another of my favourites. I once made a fire with some twigs, when Mr Mackenzie kindly left the matches lying on the ground, and I toasted some marshmallows – heavenly! The old man never left out the matches again.

I'm not sure who these kids belong to. You'd think they would be with the female, wouldn't you, but Laurel says she hasn't met them before, although that doesn't stop her making a big fuss of them, oh no! She talks to them all the time, and puts her arms around them, and then she takes a photo of them standing on either side of me. Brad doesn't care for all the attention she is giving the children – he's jealous, I do believe! He wishes she would look at *him* instead, but he doesn't know how to handle that, poor guy.

So maybe the children belong to Brad? But if so, why aren't they home with his female? He clearly hates the kids – maybe he is the father, but he doesn't know whether or not they are really his because his female doesn't know either?

Uh oh – excuse me – I'm wrong. Mr Mackenzie must be the father – he has just hit the boy on the back of the head – and no way is he joking. "I told you not to touch Laurel's camera! Why do you never listen to me, darn you?"

The poor little boy bursts into tears, but Laurel is quick to defend him. "Oh no, it doesn't matter, Mr Mackenzie! No harm done. I said he could try out my camera." That's a lie, but everyone pretends to believe it.

"Can we go outside now?" whines the little girl, who is bored. Good thing she said that – it makes everyone forget about her father's anger for now.

Me, I love going out. Our building is surrounded by woods, and there's a good picnic site down by a lake – that's my favourite place.

"Great idea," says Brad, suddenly seeing how he can get back into the limelight. "Let's have a picnic! We can get some cookies from the café and buy some cans – what drinks do you guys like?" He's trying to be nice to the children because Laurel is so taken with them.

They all go off to the café and come back with several big bags of food and drink. Somehow Mr Mackenzie is carrying most of it, and he grunts loudly with the effort. Laurel laughs – but with him, not at him – and she gives a little grunt in sympathy, which makes the old man smile. *Maybe Laurel fancies Mr Mackenzie a bit?*

The sun comes out as we reach the lake, and the kids rush down to the shore and throw off their sandals. They glance over their shoulders at the adults, but clearly they decide that someone would only tell them "no" if they stopped to ask, so they rush headlong into the water without a word. It's sandy and quite shallow, they soon discover, and they paddle up to their knees.

I'm after them at once of course, and I start splashing them, gently at first. The little girl is surprised, but the boy has started to enjoy himself and he gives me a great big splash back. *You know what, these are nice kids!*

Their father looks as if he is going to stop all this fun, but Laurel gets in first. "Come on, you guys!" She runs down to the water, and Brad works out that he will have to join in too or Laurel will stop noticing him. He wishes he'd thought of bringing my big, red plastic ball to play with – *that would have pleased the young lady, wouldn't it? Is it too late for him to go back and fetch it,* he mutters under his breath, but no one is listening.

Mr Mackenzie sighs and starts to unpack the food onto some flat stone slabs which lie just up from the shore, with the air of one who always gets left with the real work. He picks up a cookie and starts to eat it. *They haven't brought any marshmallows today – what a shame!*

After a while everyone gets hungry and we all come back to the camp. The boss makes the children sit down neatly – *yes, I think they must belong to him* – and he hands out the food. The children give me a banana of course – people always do – and I grab a can of coke, which is a favourite of mine, and tuck-in to the sandwiches. They've brought some tomato rolls and some apples.

When I've had enough to eat, I wonder if I can't liven the day up a bit. The sun is hot now, and they are all lying around not doing very much. It's so boring – *how about if I escape for a while?* So I grab the last can of coke and sprint off before anyone can get to their feet and stop me.

Brad shouts after me, but it's too late – I've slipped into the trees. They can't see where I am and of course these creatures can't smell very well. I stand quite still after a while, then I decide to shin up the tallest of the trees, some way from the camp. No one sees me.

Mr Mackenzie is shouting at Brad by now – like this is somehow Brad's fault.

"Aw, he'll be ok – keep your shirt on, Mr Mack!" Brad says, but Laurel is worried about me, and the kids want to go look for me.

Brad has an idea. "Why don't we go up to the office and get his ball? He loves playing with that in the lake – it might bring him back if he hears us splashing with it."

Laurel agrees. "What a great idea, Brad!" she says, and he goes pink in the face with pleasure. "I'll come with you." And she takes his hand.

The kids have run off into the trees, but they stick together as they search for me, calling my name. Mr Mackenzie is swearing by now, and sets off on his own in completely the wrong direction, away from everyone else, and far away from me.

I like this tree I've chosen to climb. It's got big strong branches, and it goes up a bit higher than all the other trees. There's a great view all around – I think I might stay up here for a bit. I can see right down onto the deserted camp, food still scattered around the ground; I notice the children's half eaten sandwiches, and half an apple, Laurel's camera.

In the distance I can see poor Mr Mackenzie, still walking away from here. I think he's going to trek all round the lake. He's mopping his brow and grumbling under his breath. *Where are the children? Ah, they haven't got far* – they are tired, and they are sitting on a rock by the lake now, dipping their toes into the water.

Over my shoulder I can see the path back to the office – Brad and Laurel must have gone that way to fetch my ball, but I can't see them. *Where have they got to?*

I've been up this tree for at least twenty minutes now. It's gone very quiet here, except for some bees humming and a few birds calling in the distance. *Where is everybody?*

Oh look – there's my red plastic ball! It's far away, deep among the trees where they are thickest, some distance away from the path up to the office. *What the heck is it doing there? Have they lost it?*

And then I see the two of them. The crisp white cotton blouse with three-quarter length sleeves has come off now, and so have the black jeans, abandoned on the grass. Bradley is lying on top of her, nuzzling her golden, sunburnt breasts with his tongue. She's laughing and ruffling his hair. They don't look like they are going any place soon.

Ahhhhh! That's more like it; maybe we bonobos really are their closest living relatives after all!

Now I'm going to climb down and see if I can rescue that big red plastic ball of mine.

4. Blizzard

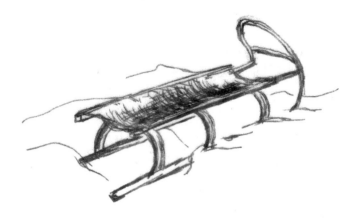

I went out to feed the birds in the back garden this morning and went flying on me bum – that icy patch by the pond – where it froze last week. Stupid thing to do; Magnus would have laughed out loud in that outrageous way he had and picked me up and dusted me down kindly.

But Magnus isn't here anymore.

Pale sunshine at the moment, but they said there was going to be more snow later on. I've still got a couple of feet of snow all around my cottage from last week's effort. I've dug out a path to the front gate, that's all. Living so high up, snow doesn't melt. To begin with it was beautiful, the stark, black trees covered in strips of white. Delicate footprints of birds all over the lawn.

The silence has been complete. No cars have come along the lane for over a fortnight – only Mac the local farmer has walked past me on his way up the hill. Mac called in with some eggs and mushrooms from his farm, which was kind of him.

I don't mind being alone up here; I've got plenty to eat for the time being – I stocked up on tins down in the village

– when it first got cold. But I do wonder how the others are getting on. The family.

Not that I see the family. Not anymore.

I still can't work out what I'm supposed to have done wrong. All I said was – and I only said this to Alan, mind – that I didn't think it was such a good idea, his wife buying that skimpy bikini with the garish flower pattern when she had put on so much weight after Felicity was born. In my humble opinion it didn't show her figure off to its best advantage – I think that's how I put it, tactful as ever.

Well, how was I to know my son was going to go and tell his wife what I had said? *Stupid pillock.*

Of course, Deborah took umbrage. Can't blame her. But there was no need for her ladyship to decree that in future Alan must never speak to me unless she, Deborah, was present. Even the children were forbidden from coming up here to see me, and it was made crystal clear that I was not welcome in their new home. Their des res, five-bedroom palace on the edge of the village, if you please.

There goes my mobile! *Someone sending me a text, I think. Now where did I put it? Ah, here we are, under the cushion on the sofa. Where are my glasses?*

"R U OK Gran?"

Oh my goodness – it's from Alice. My namesake, Alice. She must be sixteen now – I didn't see her on her last birthday, though I did post her a cheque.

I'd better reply. I'll say I'm fine, not to worry, if she is worrying.

There's another message now: "C U L8r XX"

C U? See you? Surely she doesn't expect me to walk down to the village in six foot snow drifts? Or does she mean she is coming here? I'd better check what food there is... Let's see, she's probably still vegetarian.

The phone's ringing!

Wait, wait – I'm coming, I'm coming... "Hallo?"

"Gran, is that you? It's Alice..." Sounds like Alice surrounded by a howling gale. Voice muffled.

"Where are you, darling?"

"Listen, we're coming down to see you, Gran – make sure you are alright..."

"Oh, but I'm perfectly..."

"I've got Tony with me."

"Tony?"

"My boyfriend."

"Right, I see; so where..."

Quick glance out of the window; looks pretty white out there, and the sky is leaden. No sign of that earlier sunshine.

"And Fliss is here, only she's fallen over and she won't get up."

"Oh dear."

Little Felicity is only eleven, and not the most stout-hearted of souls – when she was a toddler I was forever patching up her scrapes and cuddling away the tears. That was when we all lived in the village. I was five doors away and on call for baby-sitting duties – being a trained nurse had its advantages then.

I can hear the child sobbing in the background. Alice can be quite bossy with her younger sister, and sometimes – be fair – she does need it.

"Is she hurt, Alice?"

"Gran says, are you hurt? You're OK really, aren't you?" Pause, mumble from Felicity. "She says she's broken her ankle, Gran, and won't ever walk again... But Tony reckons it's just a sprain."

"But where are you?"

"We came up over the hill and down your lane – but we can't see where the road is meant to be – everything's

40

covered in snow. I think we've just gone past that old oak tree near the top – you know where I mean?"

Oh good heavens, that's a fair way up from my cottage.

"Have you got your sledge with you, dear?"

"No. No we left it at home when we went back for lunch. We thought we'd pop over to you this afternoon..."

"Right." Bit of quick thinking needed.

Magnus's old toboggan. Tucked away out of sight in the spare bedroom, where I keep my junk, and the rest of his stuff that I can't bear to part with.

"Stay where you are, Alice. Keep together, whatever you do. Let Fliss stay sitting down if she must. I'll be up with you in a... as soon as I can. I'll bring Granddad's toboggan with me. I won't be long..."

"Gran you're a star!"

Toboggan still in pretty good shape, thank goodness. Magnus made it himself – he was always a great carpenter. Firm, sturdy wood, with a raised metal rail round it so little children could hold on and feel safe. Must be ten years since it was last used; that day we went up to the top of the hill, and Magnus insisted on bringing a picnic of all things... but no point in thinking about that now. Work to be done: wellingtons to be struggled into, toboggan to pull.

The road isn't too bad, this first bit. Mac's footprints are here and not too hard to follow. Phew! Stop a moment. I'm alright, I'm fine, just a bit out of breath, that's all. Steep bit coming up ahead.

There they are! Huddled together on the ground, Alice with her arms around her sister. Alice jumps up and hugs me, then she turns to her boyfriend. "This is Tony, Gran."

Tony nods affably. He looks a sensible lad, at least six feet tall, a big, red scarf wrapped round half his face. He lifts Felicity onto the toboggan, makes sure she is holding onto the rail, and sets off briskly down the hill dragging it

41

behind him. In an odd way, he reminds me of Magnus when he was that age.

Alice takes my hand and we follow. It isn't so far, going down, but it seems darker now – *surely not, already?* It's hardly gone three thirty. Suddenly I realise that huge silent snowflakes are floating all round us. One lands on Alice's nose.

"Oh, not again!" I've had enough of snow.

But Alice cries out in delight. "Isn't it wonderful, Gran!"

Good thing my central heating is still working properly. I let them into the cottage and everyone stands around shaking their coats, stamping and taking off their wet boots. Tony helps Felicity onto my hall chair.

"Are your socks wet? You can put them on the radiator in the bathroom." There's a smell of steaming clothes.

Tony's socks are bright red and fluffy. "Yes, they are a bit damp," he admits as he takes them off. "My feet have been sweating!"

His feet are long and bony, and I can easily find him some of Magnus' old socks.

I turn to Felicity, who is sitting meekly on the chair. There are no more tears. "Let's have a look at this pesky ankle of yours, shall we?"

I unzip her boot and take it off – it's a struggle, but she doesn't complain – bless her. She is biting her lower lip.

"Oh yes, it is a bit swollen, isn't it?" I feel firmly all round. "But it's not broken, don't worry. Just a sprain. I can soon bandage that up for you."

Meanwhile Alice has taken Tony into the kitchen and put the kettle on.

Turns out Tony is a wizard with omelettes. Fliss sits propped up against the cupboard, her bandaged foot resting on a spare chair, happily tucking into Tony's concoction of mushroom omelette with grated cheese and what he calls his secret ingredient – he noticed the Worcester sauce at the back of the shelf. Alice is making cups of tea for everyone. As for me – why, I'm just sitting here doing nothing but beaming at the company.

Suddenly Alice's pocket begins an insistent jingle. She reaches into her jeans and pulls out her mobile. "Oh my God, it's Mum! What time is it?"

She gets up and walks into the hall, leaving the door open. Sounds as if she is trying to pacify Deborah and assuring her that they will all be home soon.

I pull the curtain aside and look out of the window, but there's nothing at all to see. Everything is completely white – even the path up to the front door is now covered in snow – indistinguishable from the banks on either side. Snowflakes are still falling, great thick ones, hundreds of them, as though snow was about to go out of fashion. Which it isn't, clearly.

Tony peers out over my shoulder. "We're not going anywhere tonight!" But he sounds quite cheerful about it.

Alice comes back into the kitchen, carrying her phone. "Dad wants to talk to you, Gran."

"Oh, right." I'm flustered as I take it from her. I haven't spoken to my son for seventeen months.

"Mum – Alan here," he barks. "Look, Alice says she's in your cottage – is everything OK? We've been worried sick down here – the wretched kids went off after lunch and never came back..."

"Yes, yes, Alan, it's alright. Tony and Alice are with me, and Felicity too..." The little girl looks up expectantly at me, but best not to mention her ankle at this point, perhaps. Deborah is already hyperventilating, I would guess. "They are fine. Tony has cooked us all a splendid tea."

"Has he now," says Alan, and I can see the purse of his lips. I know Alan so well.

"But listen, Alan – the snow has come down again – it's a proper blizzard out there. I don't know what it's like where you are, but they can't possibly leave here tonight. I'm afraid they will just have to stay! Is that all right?"

"Oh. Well I suppose it's going to have to be..."

"There's plenty of food, and plenty of room too. Don't fret, Alan. Tell Deborah she mustn't worry..."

It's been five days now.

I've found some of Magnus's old sweaters and trousers that are a good fit on Tony, and he seems pleased. The swelling on Felicity's ankle has almost gone – being forced to stay indoors for so long is the best thing that could have happened. She hopped around with my old stick for a couple of days, then she forgot the stick altogether and left it in the hall.

We've all slept reasonably well. I put Alice and Fliss together in my bed – bit of a squeeze for them but there have been no complaints. I've been sleeping in the spare room, surrounded by Magnus's junk. Made me wonder if I shouldn't sort some of it out when the snow is over and get rid of it at last. Alice says she'll help me.

Tony sleeps on the sofa, and he's always up first, getting stuff ready for breakfast. He says he could get used to evaporated milk on his cornflakes, but I doubt if I could.

On the first morning Tony built an enormous snowman in the garden, with help from Alice. It's got such a cheeky face that I offered them Magnus's battered old hat and his favourite tartan scarf for it; I even looked out his pipe. It still smells of vanilla, and Fliss says she remembers Granddad's vanilla pipe. *I'm glad she remembers him.*

"Oh Gran, that's so kind of you!" Alice said, taking me

by the arm. "Are you sure you want us to have them? They were all Granddad's!"

I hesitated before answering. "Yes. Yes of course – he would have been glad they came in useful!"

The dark evenings have been long, but we've got on pretty well – occasional squabbling over whether to watch Strictly or the X Factor, that's all; I let them sort it out amongst themselves. Tony chopped some logs for me and we built up a roaring fire in the sitting room. We've talked a lot, especially over the washing up. Alice tells me she is going to be a doctor; she wants to work in a hospital abroad during her gap year. I had no idea.

Last night the weatherman said the winds are changing and milder air is coming in from the Atlantic. It's a lot warmer this morning when I stick my nose out the back.

There's an engine noise in the lane, and as we all rush to the door we see Mac the farmer coming up – not on foot this time but in his tractor. He waves, and tells us the road down to the village is clear at last.

"You'll be able to go home," I say, gently; don't want them to think I can't wait to get rid of them.

But oddly, no one seems in a terrible hurry to leave. Fliss wants another snowball fight this morning – there's plenty of snow left – and Tony quickly obliges.

So it's nearly lunchtime when we hear another engine chugging slowly up the hill. Sounds like a four-by-four.

"It's Daddy!" Fliss recognises it first and rushes out to the lane.

But Alan is not alone, as he pulls in by my gate. It is Deborah who jumps out first and rushes up to Fliss and hugs her. Then my daughter-in-law turns to me. "Gran..."

"Hallo, dear."

"We were wondering... Will you come down with us now and stay with us for a few days? We've got a special room for you in the new house. It's really nice, garden view and everything. Please come!"

My God, she means it! I don't know what to say, but Alan sweeps past her and gives me a hug. "Of course you're coming! After you've put up with this little lot for nearly a week, it's the least…"

"Oh no, Alan – *they've* been looking after *me!*" But I go back into the cottage and look for my toothbrush.

5. A Royal Wedding

My big brother Ed went missing one Tuesday. Again... He was supposed to mow the lawn.

You know how irritating it is, when you get landed with a boring job that you really hate, just because the person who should be doing it has vanished into thin air? Well, that's how I felt that Tuesday afternoon trudging up and down the garden with our creaking old mower.

"Doesn't Ed usually do that?" Charlie asked, swinging on the gate at the end of the garden. Sometimes my cousin has no idea how annoying she is – or maybe she does it on purpose. "Where is he?"

"Not a clue," I said, pausing to wipe my brow dramatically. "Mum told me I'd better mow the lawn today, before it grows into a hayfield and people ask if they can keep their cows in our garden..."

"Well, when did you last see Ed?" Charlie doesn't let go once she gets a mystery into her head.

I stopped to think. Ed had come home from college early the day before. He'd seemed in a great hurry – he shoved me out of the way when I was trying to get a Penguin from the biscuit box, and he grabbed FIVE of them, which is like totally forbidden by Mum, who can't afford to feed us Penguins on the money she is expected to live on… Then he'd bombed upstairs into his bedroom and slammed the door shut.

"Didn't you see him at teatime, then?" Charlie asked.

Come to think of it, I hadn't seen him again. There were a few other odd things going on downstairs, and we didn't bother with Ed not being there, because Mum was frantically trying to find her hairdryer, with long, wet hair dripping everywhere.

"Well, I think we should look in Ed's bedroom," Charlie declared, getting down from the gate. "There's bound to be clues an' that to tell us where he's gone."

I was reluctant to agree. Not that I'm scared of my big brother – don't get me wrong – but last year he caught me looking through the old Lego under his bed that he doesn't play with anymore. He told me that if I ever set foot in his room again there wouldn't be any more friendly warnings, he would simply kill me. "As if there was no tomorrow," he had added casually, which I guess there wouldn't be, for me.

Ed's room was uncannily tidy. The bed was made, which was unusual, and the books on the windowsill were stacked up in a neat row – all except for one, which he'd left lying on the bed for some reason. It was an ancient copy of Hans Andersen's fairy tales that our Danish grandmother had given us when we were little.

"Oh, I know what this is!" Charlie exclaimed. "We've

48

got a copy at home. I used to love it when Mormor read it to us – you remember, Daniel!"

"But why's Ed reading it now? He said it was babyish about ten million years ago. I didn't think we still had it."

There was nothing else in Ed's room that suggested anything to us. Oh, except for a small tear in the yellow wallpaper by the door, that I'd never noticed before; looked as if a large heavy object had brushed against it. I showed it to Charlie, but we couldn't think what had caused it.

Downstairs I remembered that I was supposed to put out the green wheelie bin on the pavement after I'd cut the grass, so I went round to the garden shed to get it out – but would you believe – it wasn't there.

"Well maybe your mum has already put it out?" Charlie said. "Ours was out this morning."

I shook my head impatiently. "No, we only ever do it after everyone else."

By the evening, when Ed still didn't turn up for tea, Mum did begin to get a bit worried. She rang three or four of his mates and asked if he was staying with them, but strangely none of them seemed to have seen him.

"Oh well," she said, "he'll turn up. You don't know where he is, Daniel?"

I assured her that I didn't. She shrugged and went back to the evening paper.

It was two days before Charlie came up with her big idea.

We were sitting on a shelf in the garden shed munching olives and chocolate mini-rolls, when she produced a list of "Things That Had Gone Missing" at the same time as Ed himself:

> My Mum's winter coat
> Ed's Man United scarf
> Two whole loaves of bread

49

My alarm clock

Ed's mobile, that he always carries with him

Mum's hairdryer

The green wheelie bin

There were probably other things that no one had noticed yet.

"It's obvious, isn't it?" Charlie declared.

"Is it?"

"He must have built a time machine and gone back somewhere."

"You what???!!!"

Charlie had looked up time travel online. Just like my cousin to do that. It was quite simple, apparently, if you knew how, and she reckoned Ed was easily clever enough to have done it.

"So obviously what we've got to do," she threw in casually, "is to follow him and bring him back."

"Right…" I said, playing for time. "How, exactly?"

She'd got it all worked out. I can't believe I let myself get involved in all this, but half an hour later I found myself with Charlie in Ed's bedroom. We'd acquired another wheelie bin – the black one outside Charlie's house down the road. I think we scratched a bit of the wallpaper on the stairs when we lugged it up, but surely no one was going to notice that? It was a bit of a squeeze but we both managed to get into it, without closing the lid. A slug crept down the side as I brushed against it. Charlie had picked up a few other bits and pieces – another clock – and her dad's electric drill; I forget what else. Oh, and she said she'd be bringing her mobile with her.

"You must, too, Daniel."

I haven't got a mobile, as she very well knows, but Mum is always losing hers so it wasn't difficult to pick it up from where she'd last left it – this time it had fallen behind the bread-bin – and I slipped it into my pocket. *Sorry Mum but this may be important.* She probably wouldn't even notice.

"Where are we going?" I asked feebly.

Charlie had picked up the collection of Hans Andersen's fairy tales from Ed's bed. "I think he's gone back to old Copenhagen – say a hundred and fifty years ago? To look at some of these stories. That's where we ought to start, Daniel, somewhere near that big park we went to last year, remember? Hold tight!"

I closed my eyes. There was a big bump then, and the wheelie bin began to shift slowly across the room. I felt sick – you know the feeling you get when you're strapped into a plane that's just going to take off? It starts slowly, then goes faster and faster like a crazy car on a speed track, then suddenly the plane's nose tilts up, and your feet go up into space while your stomach tries hard to keep up. I always hate it.

"It's working, Daniel!" Charlie grabbed my arm with excitement.

"Yeah, OK." I just wanted it all to be over – quickly, if possible.

It took hours, at least that's how it felt to me, but Charlie says it was only a few minutes. I felt a heavy thud as we came down, and she scrambled out. I caught my leg on the side of the wheelie bin, but I managed to follow her. I took a deep breath and looked around.

It was a dark night and bitterly cold – there was snow on the ground. We were in a narrow, cobbled street with high buildings all around us. There were hardly any people about – I should think they'd all hurried home to get out of the cold. A couple of women in long coats came past with a man in a top hat. We saw a Christmas tree with bright decorations in a square at the end of the street.

51

In the distance we noticed a church with a tall spire that had an outside staircase curling all round it, which Charlie recognised. "Oh look, Daniel," she cried, "there's that spire we went up last summer! *Vor Frelsers Kirke*. We must really be in Copenhagen."

"Wow!" I said. My cousin knew what she was doing, after all.

We walked along the street and came to an alleyway where a girl was standing. She must have been absolutely frozen because she was in bare feet, with only a thin dress and nothing on her head. She had a tray of matches hanging round her neck.

"Hallo," she said. "Do you want to buy some matches?" She must have spoken in Danish, but we seemed to understand her.

"No thank you," said Charlie politely. "Not today. Sorry..." she added, as a small tear began to trickle down the girl's face.

The child sniffed and rubbed her nose with her sleeve. "I haven't sold any matches today – it's New Year's Eve and everyone is in such a hurry to get home. They don't want magic matches."

"Why don't you go home, then?" I asked, thinking this might well be a stupid question.

It was. The girl told us that she would be beaten if she went back without selling any matches. She struck a match against the wall of the alley, and suddenly it flared up so that we could see a picture of a great palace shining in the dark, with Christmas decorations all around the outside. "I wish I lived there!" she said. "They have plenty to eat and they never have to sell matches."

"Where is it?" I gasped.

"Oh, I know," said Charlie. "It's Amalienborg palace – we've been there. Tell you what, why don't you come with us? We are looking for my cousin so we might as well start at the palace. You can leave your matches here – no one will take them."

The child agreed with relief, and Charlie took her hand as we hurried through the streets to the palace. As we turned the corner, we saw an old man standing outside, looking up and down the road as though he was waiting for someone.

"You people," he called out to us. "You haven't seen my son, have you? The prince? We had a message that he was coming back tonight. He's been all over the world looking for a Real Princess to marry, but he says he hasn't had any success yet."

Charlie's face lit up. She nudged me and muttered something about how she remembered that story. So did I, vaguely – was it something about a pea?

"No, I'm afraid we haven't seen your son, sire," Charlie said. "But we have come to the palace tonight because we have just rescued Princess Bodil and we thought you would want to welcome her."

"What's that you say?" the old man said.

The girl stared.

"The poor thing was set upon by a gang of thugs who stole all her money – she was travelling with a great chest full of gold," Charlie told him. She does tell a good story, does my cousin. "And they took all her fine clothes and left her lying in a ditch in just these rags! That's where my cousin and I found her. She was coming to visit you."

"Oh, good heavens, how dreadful! You must come in at once, my dear. I'll get my wife the queen…"

As he turned away and frantically began to ring the bell hanging by the door, Charlie whispered to the girl. "Now listen, child. This is dead important, and I'm only going to say it once, so listen good." Charlotte put her hands on the girl's shoulders. "They will give you a lovely warm bed for the night, but tomorrow morning when they ask you if you have slept well, you must say that you didn't sleep a wink – not one wink, understand? Because there was something there, under all the mattresses, that stopped you resting properly. OK?"

The child nodded dumbly, and the last we saw of her was when the old king ushered her into the palace and closed the door.

Charlie rubbed her hands. "That went well, didn't it? Though I say so myself…"

"Yes brilliant," I agreed. "She's a princess for life. But what about us, Charlie? It doesn't exactly help us find Ed. Now what do we do?"

That's when I had my own moment of brilliance. "We could phone him," I went on.

"Course we could – I was just going to say that," Charlie said, whipping out her mobile from her pocket and scrolling down for his number. "It's ringing, Daniel!"

It rang for some time, then we heard a clipped voice saying, "Who's that?" Unmistakably my brother.

"Ed, where are you?" my cousin cried. "It's Charlie here, and Daniel. We've come to find you."

There was a pause, then he said, "I'm at the harbour. I've got something going on here – my partner's a tailor. Look, I don't want any interference…"

"Your partner?" cried Charlie. "What on earth are you on about, Ed?"

There was a sharp click, and he hung up.

"We know the way to the harbour, Daniel – remember, we went there last year. Come on!" Charlie doesn't hang about, and I hurried to keep up with her as we ran through the old, cobbled streets. They looked familiar of course, but without the big modern glass buildings that I expected to see here and there.

Soon we got to Nyhavn, a little inlet of sea like a finger sticking into the land, lined with old buildings where last summer my mother had discovered a restaurant which did the most heavenly lobster. They'd given me fish fingers.

"That anchor's not there!" I exclaimed. There should have been a big, iron sculpture of an anchor at the head of the inlet, but obviously it hadn't been made yet. As this dawned on me, the hairs on the back of my neck prickled.

"Never mind that, Daniel. Look, there he is, down the far end…"

I saw where she was pointing, and there indeed was my brother, standing outside one of the buildings – surely the very same one where Mum had had that lobster last year? He was talking to a shifty looking bloke wearing a cowboy hat, who didn't look in the least like a tailor. We raced along by the water.

"What the hell are you two doing here?" Ed turned and snarled at us. "I told you, I'm busy!"

"What's happening?" I panted, out of breath and sounding rather lame even to myself.

The cowboy turned and said, quite politely, "We have rented this building. We are taking orders for making clothes of the most magical kind…"

Ed dug him in the ribs. "Shut up, Svend!"

My brother started shouting at us that we ought to go away, fast, using quite a few of the words that Mum doesn't let me use, but as his voice washed over me I suddenly knew what was going on: they were going to make clothes that could only be seen by VERY CLEVER PEOPLE. Wasn't there some king who was going to order them, and then when the clothes were only pretend ones, no one would be brave enough to say that they couldn't see them because that would be admitting that they were stupid? Even the king himself wouldn't be able to see the clothes because they simply didn't exist, but he couldn't let on that he was too dim to be a king.

"Come on, Daniel," Charlie said, taking my hand. "Let's go!"

We ran back through the streets. It was very dark and I couldn't remember which way we'd come – what if we couldn't find the wheelie bin that we'd arrived in? How would we ever get back home? A very small feeling started off in my stomach and slowly spread upwards and outwards – panic!

"It was somewhere along the middle of Strøget, wasn't it? Must have been," she said.

I had absolutely no idea, so I kept quiet. We soon came to a big square with a bare, wintry tree which Charlie said was Kongens Nytorv.

"That's right, I remember now!" she cried. "Come on, Strøget's down this way."

At last we turned a bend in the narrow street and saw the old black wheelie bin, mercifully still there, lying on its side. *Phew!* We scrambled into it and Charlie did whatever it was that she'd worked out to make the thing go. *I'll have to find out some time how she does it.* I closed my eyes and pinched my nose the way you do on planes to stop your ears hurting.

As we landed with a small bump back in Ed's bedroom, the mobile in my pocket began to vibrate. Someone had sent Mum a message.

"It's from Ed," I told my cousin. "He says 'no worries Mum have gone to Cornwall back next week'. What on earth is he playing at?"

We didn't know anyone in Cornwall. He was lying to stop Mum worrying, obviously. We left Mum's mobile on the kitchen table for her to see.

Mum was in an unusually good mood at teatime. "A boy

of eighteen is quite old enough to look after himself," she declared, scooping some chips out of the pan. She'd got a job interview the next day, and she'd borrowed a hairdryer from Charlie's mother.

"We'll just have to go back, Daniel," Charlie said that evening. Somehow, I'd been expecting that.

"Right," I said cautiously.

"He's still there, in Copenhagen – we'll have to persuade him to come home. Come on, let's fetch the wheelie bin."

It was different this time; maybe I wasn't so scared. We landed in broad daylight, and I realised straight away that it wasn't cold; it was a pleasantly warm spring day. We were in a large park, by the looks of it, and several horse-drawn carriages were ambling along with passengers taking the air.

"I know where we are!" Charlie cried. "We're near the palace – come on – let's go and find our little match girl and see what's happened to her."

We parked the wheelie bin under a bush and set out. A few people stared at us – I guess our clothes were different from everyone else's – but Charlie took my arm and hurried me along.

When we came to the royal palace, there was a sentry standing outside a box. He had a rifle over his shoulder, and a big black bearskin hat and a red uniform so he looked just like those pictures in children's books.

Charlie went straight up to him. "Hallo," she said brightly. "Can you tell me how we can find Princess Bodil?"

He had to tilt his bearskin hat back on his head before he could see us properly – I've always wondered how they manage that. "What? You haven't seen the relief column of soldiers come to take over sentry duty, have you? Only my feet are killing me, and I haven't had a cup of tea since breakfast."

"Oh dear, I'm so sorry," Charlie said politely. "I'm afraid we haven't seen any other soldiers. We are looking for Princess Bodil – do you know who I mean?"

He threw back his head and laughed. "Know who you mean? I should think I do! The whole kingdom knows about Princess Bodil. The newspapers write about nothing else... My wife and daughters cut out everything they can lay their hands on. What she wore at the races, what she wears when she pops over to Tivoli. What she's going to wear on the Big Day..."

"Really?"

"Well, it's such a long time since we last had a royal wedding, isn't it? The whole country has gone mad. You must have noticed, unless you've just arrived from another planet!"

"Oh yes we know all about that," I put in quickly. "We're reporters with the Copenhagen Evening Post – it's a new evening paper – you might have seen it? We've got an appointment to see her today. We are writing a piece about the wedding. We just wondered which gate we're supposed to go to."

Charlie turned to me with a look of admiration which I still treasure.

At that moment the gate opened and an elderly woman came out carrying a mug of tea.

"At last!" the soldier cried, tilting his helmet even further back and seizing his drink.

"Sorry Poul – there's chaos inside, I couldn't come sooner. His Majesty is going on about these new tailors he's found. Supposed to be some sort of magic. Load of rubbish, if you ask me!"

"They won't ask you, though, will they?" said the sentry

with a wink, and he drank his tea in one go. "Here, can you take these good folk in and find the princess? They are reporters. Play your cards right, and they might write a piece about you!"

She peered at us. "Funny clothes reporters wear nowadays! Well, you'd better follow me."

So we did.

We found Princess Bodil in her bedroom trying on her wedding dress in front of a floor-length mirror.

"What do you think?" she asked us. "It's deadly secret of course, but you won't let on, will you? I can trust you two…"

She obviously remembered us, although she herself looked years older – she wasn't the little match girl we'd found in the dark, cold Christmas season – but a young woman now, about Ed's age. There must be something very peculiar about this time travel stuff.

Charlie gasped. "It's – it's – amazing," she said tactfully. "I love all those flouncy bits hanging from the waist…"

"Flouncy bits," I echoed lamely. As far as I could see, it was just a long white dress which might prove a bit impractical if you were wearing it for any length of time, or trying to do something useful like cycling to the park to meet your mates or mowing the lawn. Wish I'd thought of getting into a wedding dress when Mum made me mow the lawn, come to think of it.

"I'm not supposed to show anyone – I'd better take it off." She sounded reluctant.

"Don't look, Daniel," said Charlie sternly as Princess Bodil slipped out of the dress and put on an ordinary brown one. So I gazed out of the window and watched some soldiers marching up and down. They were probably practising for the Royal Wedding.

"It's lovely to see you again," Bodil went on as she bundled the wedding dress into the wardrobe and turned the key. "I didn't think I ever would." She turned to us with a big smile. "I'll order some tea for us, shall I?"

The tea came on a gilt tray with elegant china. Charlie nudged me and said, "Watch out, Daniel – it's Copenhagen porcelain. For God's sake don't drop anything!"

I realised that I was actually quite hungry. There were some rather cool looking pastries.

"So tell us all about the wedding, Bodil!" Charlie said as we attacked the food. "What's the prince like?"

"He's OK when we are alone," she said. "He's funny – he makes me laugh, and I think he really does love me…"

"But?" said Charlie.

"But his family are a bit scary. His mother is terribly strict, and his father gets these funny ideas. Have you heard the latest?"

I sat up. "You don't mean magic tailors?"

"That's right," she said. "It's a mad idea! All the other men in the family are going to wear military uniforms for the wedding. The prince is getting medals specially made, and his uncle has his whole breast full of metalware, but not the king."

Charlie and I glanced at each other. "We've got to stop him, Daniel."

"I can help you," Bodil said eagerly. "He's not letting anyone into his office at the moment, because he's so busy with these awful new clothes, but he likes me. He'll listen if I tell him I want to come and talk to him. Maybe tomorrow afternoon would be a good time, when he comes in from hunting in the royal park… He'll be in a good mood then."

I glanced at Charlie. *How could we possibly stay until tomorrow afternoon? Mum would go nuts.*

"I think it would be OK," Charlie said slowly. "I've worked out a way of changing the timings so that when we go back we won't be more than a few hours past the time we left."

Awesome.

"But hang on, why didn't Ed do that?" I went on.

Charlie didn't know; *maybe Ed was planning to stay on a lot longer – why else would he want to make a fortune out of cheating people? Did he want to stay on and actually live here?* My stomach felt cold.

"Oh, please stay!" begged Princess Bodil – I think the poor kid was lonely. "You can sleep in the palace – there are loads of spare rooms. But first I'd better give you some better clothes. If you go round dressed in that peculiar way, people will wonder who you are. Much better that nobody notices you."

She was right of course. I must say it felt odd, putting on a suit with a high collar, but Charlie – who normally wears nothing but jeans and a tee shirt and a pair of ancient trainers – said she could quite get used to the long dress Bodil found for her.

The next day the king cancelled his hunting trip in the royal park. By the time Bodil took us over to his office, he was already up there, and his personal assistant told us that he had strict instructions that no one should be allowed in.

"Oh, that's alright," Bodil said airily. "He won't mind me coming up. He asked me to come round this afternoon." I wasn't sure if that was strictly true, but Bodil gave the poor man one of her angelic smiles and he couldn't stop her. My cousin and I ran after her up the stairs before he could change his mind.

Bodil burst open the door and strode in. We followed, leaving the door open behind us.

There was the old king, looking rather tubby in a pair of knickerbockers, I suppose you'd call them, and some yellow and purple striped stockings; I don't think they had boxer shorts in those days. And nothing else.

He was staring at himself in a mirror which was being helpfully held up for him by – yes, you guessed it – my brother Ed. His so-called partner was standing by the window looking at them with a smirk on his face.

The king jumped out of his skin. "What… what's going on? Who are these people?"

"They are my friends, Your Majesty," Bodil told him. They are called Charlie and Daniel, and they wanted to come and see the new clothes you have ordered for the wedding."

She actually curtsied at that point.

Ed turned and gave us a look of pure poison.

"So, when are you going to try out the clothes?" Bodil asked innocently. "We'd love to see."

The king took a deep breath, glanced at Ed, then said slowly, "I am trying them on. Can't you see, girl?"

No one said anything for what seemed about a week, then I cleared my throat.

"Actually, Your Majesty, you haven't got any clothes on. Apart from your boxers, of course. Sorry, I mean your knickerbockers, Sire. And your stockings are class…"

No one moved. Then suddenly Ed dropped the mirror and bolted towards the open door. His partner overtook him and escaped, but Charlie grabbed Ed's legs as he went past so that he came crashing to the floor.

"Gerrof, Charlie! Leave me alone…" My brother thrashed about and hit Charlie across the face, but she wouldn't let go.

"Guards! Guards, quick – arrest this man!" shouted the king.

It took three of them to pin him down, but in the end they got hold of him and began to march him towards the door. He turned round and stared at me with a look of – *what?* He wasn't furious anymore. I saw the beginnings of panic on his face, and he pleaded for help. But I had no idea what I could do, and he was led away.

In the end it was Charlie who persuaded the king to let Ed go, on condition that we took him home with us and never let him anywhere near this place again. The king insisted that Ed should stay in the dungeon under the palace until Charlie and I were ready to leave – he wasn't taking any chances.

But we weren't about to leave just yet – we had to stay on for the wedding of course. Princess Bodil insisted, and it seemed only polite.

She looked pretty good – radiant, Charlie tells me I'm supposed to say – and she was the star of the show, obviously, but I couldn't help noticing the old king. He wore the uniform of a ten-star general, bright scarlet, and attracted quite a lot of attention. As he processed down the aisle after the ceremony, arm in arm with the queen, he turned when he came level with us. He looked me straight in the eye, gave a wry smile and then – just for a moment – I could have sworn that he winked at me.

6. Fresh Beginnings

To the Chief Executive,
Sainsbury's UK

Dear Sir/Madam – well I expect you are a Sir rather
than a Madam – gender inequality at the top of our
great retail companies being what it manifestly is –
so Dear Sir, (sorry no time to Google your actual
name but you will know what it is, no doubt).

It has come to my attention that your Sketty
branch in Swansea is in need of upgrading and
substantial reorganisation. I should like to offer my
services.

Let me introduce myself. My name is Matilda
Moraghan (Please note the "g" in the spelling of my
name – so many people don't, and it drives me
potty...) and I am a qualified specialist in Artificial
Intelligence and Systems Analysis. I would like to
present you with my radical new plans for this modest
little branch. First, I would tear down all the aisles
and clear the space for genuine interaction between

the buying public (the punters) and your staff, many of whom would sadly have to be let go at this point.

The goods would be stacked neatly along the back wall of the store, a wall which I would first pull down and rebuild ten yards further back to afford more space. I would change the order in which goods are stacked, so that (for example) Bovril is next to Marmite, rather than some irritating distance away from it; they do after all serve much the same purpose. Unless of course you are a vegetarian, which, as it happens, I am not.

I have several more radical ideas which would vastly improve your footfall, but before I go into these, I should clear up a couple of points: my remuneration and my availability.

I have been accustomed to commanding six-figure salaries to date, and naturally I could not contemplate taking over your store for anything less. I am open to offers, but I should point out that a few other retail outfits are interested in me, here and in the United States. (Waitrose have asked me not to mention their name.)

As for my availability, I am committed to finishing my work at a new Aldi store in Cardiff, and they have indicated that they would find it impossible to carry on without me. This should take three more months. After that, I have promised my grandchildren Gruff and Ori that I will take them to Alton Towers, a trip that will have to fit in with their parents' holiday plans, so I cannot say when it will be possible. Once that trip is accomplished, I am all yours!

I look forward to hearing from you urgently.

Yours faithfully,

Dr Matilda Moraghan

To the Secretary,
International Tiddlywinks / Netball team
Malawi

Dear Sir,

I am writing to apply for the post of coach for your international team, which I understand is vacant. I am currently living in Swansea, UK but I shall very shortly be obliged to relocate to Malawi, as my sister Dr Matilda Moraghan is being pursued by an entirely mistaken and unjust legal process involving matters too tedious to bore you with.

So the two of us are arriving in your beautiful country next Thursday. We shall initially have the status of temporary visitors, but once you have accepted me as your netball coach – no sorry, do I mean tiddlywinks coach? – I trust that we will both be granted work permits and given leave to remain indefinitely. I assume that is how it works? This has been arranged in somewhat of a hurry, and we have not had time to investigate the status of overseas professionals in Madagascar / Malawi.

As you may well be aware, I can claim in all modesty to be a world champion in your sport. I realise that your team has not had much international success so far in competitions – frightfully bad luck being beaten by Germany on penalties last year! Or was it Switzerland? Whatever. A demoralizing experience I'm sure, and one for which you have my deepest sympathy. But fear not, I have just the right qualities to put this right. I am hardworking and steady, and very good at bonding a team together. I tend to model myself on Gareth Southgate. Furthermore, I am athletic, and used to running and

66

jumping, and excellent at shooting goals through a net – though that might not be quite so necessary in the case of tiddlywinks, I admit.

My sister Dr Moraghan wants me to add that she too would be happy to work for you if a suitable post should offer itself. She has many qualities; she has been working in retail, so perhaps she could run your team gift shop? She too is hard working and steady, and used to running and jumping... Perhaps more pertinently, she has excellent business sense, as well as being honest and above all modest. She has some interesting ideas on how to market key rings and stationery items with your national flag printed on them. What striking colours you have on your flag! And perhaps with pictures of your animals – maybe lemurs, or crocodiles, if you have any in your beautiful land? She is also very good at drawing tigers. Do you have penguins, I wonder?

If we have not received your reply before we leave the UK, you can find us at the Best Western Hotel in Nairobi – possibly Accra? I'm sorry for the confusion; this will all be sorted out when we arrive in your wonderful country. We are very keen on mountains – but also of course flat plains; we love the sea, but naturally we do not mind being far from the coast.

With very best wishes,
Gerard Moraghan BA in Sports Science

To Her Majesty the Queen
London, UK

Dear Ma'am – I do hope that is the correct way to address you – I am writing to introduce myself and

my extremely talented sister Dr Matilda Moraghan.
We have heard that you are in need of a new head
gardener in your wonderful gardens, and we should
like to offer our services.

We are currently residing in Malawi but we shall
very shortly be concluding our business here. I have
been coaching the national lacrosse team in Malawi
with some moderate success. (You will no doubt be
aware that lacrosse was first played as early as the
seventeenth century – though not of course in Malawi!
It is not in fact all that different from polo, which
several members of your own family are proficient
at ... Except that lacrosse players do not ride horses, of
course. Maybe they should ...) Unfortunately the
World Lacrosse Championship has been unfairly
dominated of late by other more powerful countries
and our employers here in Lilongwe feel that they no
longer have the resources to pay the salaries of my
sister and myself. In short, they have asked us to leave
on the next available flight.

Luckily this leaves us free to apply to run your
gardens, beginning with the one surrounding
Buckingham Palace. I know that you have a vast
array of very old plants there, and no doubt you will
want to keep some of these for sentimental reasons –
those planted by Queen Victoria and her consort for
example – your distinguished forebears. However I
wonder if we could introduce some more modern
foliage? We are hoping to bring over to the UK some
of the fascinating plants we have seen here in
Malawi, although we anticipate that there may be
some minor export regulations to overcome. Fear
not, my sister Matilda, who is as you will be aware a
world-famous botanist, has a special compartment in

her suitcase which should remain safely hidden from the prying eyes of the customs officials. I believe we can promise you a wide variety of plants native to Malawi, such as the many orchid species – more here than in any other African country.

It would be most convenient if you could reply to this letter by return. Could you also ask your Foreign Secretary (I forget who it is at present, but you will no doubt know) to make it plain to the authorities in Malawi that my sister and I are BRITISH SUBJECTS and should not be in any way harassed or indeed IMPRISONED. If you could also send us the return fare to London, it would be greatly appreciated.

Yours most sincerely,

Gerard Moraghan BA, Fellow of the Royal College of Gardeners, Dip Ed

To the Chief Education Officer
South Wales

Dear Madam,

I am replying to your advert for a qualified person to run play schemes over the Christmas holidays in your area. You may have come across my work already in connection with my reorganisation of the little Sainsbury's in Sketty. Since my work there, my brother Gerard and I have been abroad on a secret assignment for Her Majesty's government which naturally I am not at liberty to disclose to you, but I can tell you that Her Majesty was so grateful for our help in this matter that she invited us to supervise the development of aspects of her beloved garden at Buckingham Palace. I am of course a qualified botanist, as you will know.

69

With the coming of the autumn, the Queen has graciously indicated that our work for her is complete. We both expect to be suitably rewarded in the New Year Honours List – a knighthood for my brother is not beyond the bounds of possibility – and for myself, Dame Matilda would seem to have a certain ring to it, would it not? But that is strictly under wraps for now, and we are sure we can rely on your discretion.

We find ourselves therefore at liberty to offer our services to you to run play schemes over the Christmas holidays. (It was Christmas, not Easter, wasn't it? I'm afraid I can't at the moment put my finger on the advert my brother showed me.)

We are, both of us, eminently suited to working with children of all ages. I have practically brought up my grandchildren Ori and Gruff, and I know all about Fortnite (which Gruff tells me is the correct spelling – he has a tee-shirt to prove it), Minecraft, Pepper Pig et al – what a wealth of entertainment our modern youth is heir to! Gruff and Ori go to holiday play schemes quite often, but I have found what is on offer rather pedestrian up till now. My ideas would be far more ambitious; my brother Gerard is of course a well-known round-the-world yachtsman, and I would like to introduce an element of adventure for children. We would organise a yacht race along the Bristol Channel from Dale in the west to Caldicot in the east; you would have to provide the yachts, with the cost for each child reflecting the cost of hiring suitable boats.

Another possibility would be a televised cookery competition – they are all the rage these days, aren't they? I have worked as a chef myself in the past – my work for Harrods was particularly successful when my creation entitled "Caramel Latte Matilda" won an award on a national show. I have connections with S4C, the BBC and ITV Wales and would be able to pull a few strings.

We have several more ideas which we would like to run before you. Please do get in touch without delay as I am also being considered for the post of Chief Assistant to the Secretary General of the United Nations.

Yours cordially,
Dame (almost) Matilda Moraghan

To the Editor,
Western Mail

Sir,

I wish to deny in the strongest possible terms the slanderous claim by the Chief Executive of Sainsbury's worldwide that I had any causal involvement in the enforced closure of the little Sainsbury's store in Gower Road, Sketty and its replacement with a branch of the Co-op. I assure you and all your discriminating readers that this was in no way a result of the imaginative and far-sighted work I did there a few years ago when I replaced all the aisles with open-plan marketing.

My solicitor will be handling this matter with the greatest of urgency.

I wonder sometimes if my time is yet to come.
Yours,
Matilda Moraghan (Ms)

7. Damage

We thought we'd got away with it – yeah!

But look – what's this letter on the doormat, sticking out ominously under the special offers from Asda and two postcards from Mum's friend in Weightwatchers? French stamp – bit of a clue there, I would have thought. Mum's name and address typed on it: Mrs D V N Phillips, exactly as it says on her credit card.

But we've already been home four days – came back to London last Sunday on Eurostar.

It's a sunny day in early July, already hot, full of promise – and no one is hassling me to do anything. I was planning to chill out with my mates, if anyone is around. I need a letter from a French car hire company like I need a pile of shit in the kitchen.

It surely is from the car hire people, though. Their address is on the front – Hertz, Nîmes, La France. *No pressure there, then. What are they writing to Mum for now? Come to think of it, it did seem too easy, returning the hire car at Nîmes last Saturday. Suspiciously easy.* My sister Sarah just parked the shiny, green Citroen in the car park, sauntered into the office and handed over the keys.

Maybe Mum signed something – I don't remember. And that was it; they didn't even come out into the car park to look at the car.

Maybe they have had a look since.

Mum's in work already of course – she leaves the house at ten to eight sharp. Sometimes I hear her bang the front door, but if I'm lucky I just turn over and go back to sleep. *After all the slog I put into my A Levels this summer I deserve it.*

Nothing I can do about the letter so might as well go and get some breakfast. I put it down carefully on the hall table to await Mum's return from work. *I need music: think I'll put some Coldplay on in the kitchen.* My girlfriend Annie gave me a CD of X & Y just before my holiday, and I haven't had a chance to hear it yet.

I'm just pouring out some orange juice when there's a beep from my mobile – *who's this?* Text from my friend Will – but he's meant to be away still with his parents. Short and sweet: "R U OK?" he says. *That's a no brainer – why wouldn't I be?* I tuck my mobile back in my pocket – I'll answer him later.

What if the hire company did look more closely at the green Citroen – what would they see? Just a few odd scratches, perhaps – but that was hardly our fault.

That great big stone wall opposite the hotel, the slight slope down to the river… We stayed in this amazing old hotel in a village called Valleraugue, deep in the countryside west of Nîmes. The idea was to meet up with Mum's American cousin George, who was over from the States with his two little kids. George rented a cottage just outside the village and we went out with them a few times; he's taken them up to Paris this week, though I doubt if his children will appreciate the city.

George's children are pretty lively – there's Rosie-Lee, who is nine, and her little brother Mickey, who is four. We tried smuggling them into the outdoor swimming pool at our hotel, but they made too much noise jumping in and splashing each other in their endearing American way when the hotel had a wedding party going on, and the concierge got very angry and shouted at us to get out of the pool and go away. I'm the only one who actually speaks French, so I paraphrased what she was saying to avoid upsetting the children. We abandoned the pool and decided to drive off to the seaside instead.

Just across the road from the hotel was the river. It was wide and flat there, so you kept forgetting there was a slight dip down from the road – and the way to it was blocked by this big grey stone wall. Mum was the first person to go forwards into it, when she was struggling to get into reverse on the first morning.

"Damn this bloody car – why can't they put reverse in a sensible place?" Mum went on to give us the colourful version of her car-related vocabulary.

But when Sarah and I looked at the front of the car, it really was only a tiny scratch where Mum had inched her way into the wall – *no one would notice it, surely?*

Think I'll make myself a couple of slices of toast, with plenty of butter; great, Mum's left the marmalade out.

Maybe I ought to ring Sarah at her work and see what she thinks about the letter?

She answers at once. "It's ever so quiet in here," she says. "It's really weird, Jake. No one's in the office this morning."

"Oh?"

"One guy is away on holiday, I know, but there are two other people who should be here and they haven't turned

74

up. I was with them both yesterday and they never said a word..."

"Right." I can't throw any light on that for her, so I go on, "Listen, Sarah – Mum's had a letter from the car hire people in Nîmes..."

"Oh my God. What does it say?"

"Well, I haven't stooped to steaming open Mum's letters yet... But it's pretty obvious, isn't it? They've, like, found one or two small blemishes on their precious car and they are going to charge Mum."

"Never! Can they do that, Jake?"

"Sure can. It was in the original agreement, don't you remember? They took a copy of Mum's credit card, or whatever, and they can go on taking cash off it."

"What, even now? But we've handed back the vehicle!"

"Doesn't matter, Sarah. They can still charge Mum's card. She can't stop them. And she is not going to be best pleased, I would have thought."

"It wasn't all me!" My sister laughs like a peal of bells, reverberating in her empty office. "But never mind, it was a great holiday, wasn't it?"

"It had its moments," I admit. "Remember that time when we all went to the Grotte des Demoiselles, and George suddenly appeared on that rock shelf above the cave waving his arms and declaiming about how the world was created the night before Sunday 23rd October 4004 BC? Embarrassing, or what?"

The Grotte des Demoiselles is a huge ancient cave system full of awesome stalagmites and stalactites, thousands of years old. Rosie-Lee and Mickey found it scary, and we had to keep a tight hold of their hands when we went on the guided tour, especially when their father mysteriously disappeared.

"Oh, he was only joking!" Sarah says. "George doesn't really think that. He was just showing off. Jake..."

"What?"

"You don't think it made any difference, do you? When we drove away from the Grotte we were in a hurry because you and George had already left and he had an idea for a good place to eat that night..."

I had swapped cars at that point – I went in George's car with the kids because they needed someone to cheer them up and make them laugh, while Sarah and Mum followed us.

"Why, what happened?"

"I got kind of hooked up with another car when I was trying to leave the Grotte..." Now she tells me.

"What!"

"Well, more of a Land Rover, really. It was their fault – I think they admitted it. They both got out of their car and shouted at me."

This is news to me.

"In French?"

"Well yes of course in French. We were in France, weren't we? An elderly man – about forty – and a dead glamorous woman."

"And you didn't understand a word they said, did you?"

"Not as such, no. But it was only the two bumpers..." She sounds proud of this.

"The bumpers?"

"That's what bumpers are for, isn't it, Jake?" There's a small pause. "What? You're not saying anything, Jake."

"I'm speechless." I swallow. "How much damage was it?"

"Oh, nothing... hardly anything at all. Just a few scratches at the back, just below the bumper. You didn't even notice, did you?"

"I wasn't looking, was I?"

There's a sound from her end of the line. "Oh thank

goodness – someone's coming at last – I'll have to go. Talk to you later, Jake. Listen, tell me when Mum opens the letter, yeah?"

We ring off and I pour myself a mug of tea.

Here comes another text message – cool, it's my girlfriend. "Are you safe?" she says mysteriously. Unlike Will, Annie doesn't believe in text-speak, but hey, the meaning is the same. *What the hell is going on here? Why is everyone suddenly concerned about my well-being?*

She has gone up to Scotland, to this place called Gleneagles, to demonstrate at the G8 Summit about Africa and global warming. She's hoping Tony Blair will pull something off, but she isn't holding her breath. I'm expecting her to text me about what's going on up there today – the summit began yesterday, and she sent me several messages in the evening.

Oh dear; the extra news from my sister is bad. Sounds a lot more violent than what Mum did – and me, a couple of times, I must admit – going forward into that damn wall instead of getting into reverse. At this point I ought to confess that there was another small incident, although to be fair only the wheel hub was affected. Just a little.

Me, I blame the ladybird.

Of course, it was George's idea to speed along the autoroute after we left Avignon. He said it would be faster, and paying the toll would be gravy.

But getting out of Avignon was the first problem. We'd parked in this enormous underground car park, spread out below the papal palace. No idea where. There were several entrances up to the surface, obviously, and they all looked the same. Quaint, little French-type buildings in quaint, little French-type streets – but which one had we come up out of?

It was a seriously hot day. We had made the kids traipse round this vast building looking at statues and paintings which Mum and Sarah claimed they were interested in. The shouting began when Rosie-Lee put her sticky paws on a horse that some pope was sitting on; Rosie-Lee likes horses – in fact back home in the States I'm told she rides one. But the museum guard didn't rate Rosie-Lee's interest in this horse, especially when he realised that she had been eating strawberry ice-cream which she had not quite finished. He let loose a torrent of French and started waving his arms around – understandably perhaps – and Rosie-Lee and Mickey both burst into tears.

At that point George and I decided to take them off for a boat trip on the river, which was OK except that we nearly drowned Mickey when he tried climbing up the side of the boat, and George had to teach them to sing *Sur Le Pont D'Avignon* to calm them down.

"Where is the bridge? Can we see it?" Rosie-Lee had demanded.

But the famous pont is a bit of a let-down – it only goes halfway across the river, which I would have thought made it slightly less than useful as a bridge.

We met up with Mum and Sarah, and managed to get some lunch. We even found something that Mickey would eat – I forget what; that child lives on crisps, usually – and then we set off to find our two cars. George found his at once of course.

He phoned us a couple of times when we were still looking for ours, and gave us directions on how to get out of Avignon on the A7, the autoroute. All we had to do was simply follow him, he said. Gravy, he said.

"Yeah, right," I told him, wondering if we would ever get out of this underground maze. I may have become slightly agitated at this point.

In the end Mum spotted a bright yellow Renault and remembered that, because it was her favourite colour, she'd noticed it on the end of the row where we had put our car. This time she was right, there was our Citroen, nestling in a corner as if butter wouldn't melt. We fell into it.

Don't ask me which entrance I drove out of. We got straight into a confusing tangle of fast roads, all with confident French traffic zipping along.

Sarah phoned George.

"Where the hell are you?" he had demanded. "We've been waiting half an hour for you!"

"Er... Not quite sure," she had admitted. "There's a big grey building over on the right, I think... Are you anywhere near that?"

Wisely he ignored that remark. "Look Sarah, it's gravy. All you do is find the road south... Like I told you an hour ago, the A7. You'll find it advertised in BIG LETTERS up above the road."

Half an hour later, or it may have been a little longer, we finally came round the same roundabout for the tenth time and saw Rosie-Lee and Mickey sitting on a grass verge eating a bar of chocolate.

"There they are!" Mum shouted, causing me to swerve into the next lane of traffic. "Pull in, Jake!"

A couple of other drivers hooted. I would have hooted back if I could have remembered how.

It was not long afterwards, when we were cruising along behind George towards the toll road, that the ladybird joined us. Suddenly I saw it walking ever so slowly across the windscreen outside the car, just in front of my nose.

"Oh look, Jake – there's a ladybird!" Sarah is keen on insects. "Cool! How on earth did it get there?"

"No idea." It was mesmerising. The faster we drove, the slower the poor thing walked, until it came to a halt altogether, stuck in the middle and wondering what the hell was going on.

"Isn't that supposed to be lucky?" Mum asked.

"If it flaps its wings here, doesn't that cause a hurricane in America?" Sarah said.

"No, you're thinking of butterflies," I told her.

The ladybird was still with us when we got to the tollbooth onto the autoroute.

"It's a piece of cake…" That was George, on the phone to us again. For some reason he had picked up the idea that I might not know what to do at a French tollbooth. "Just press the button and pick up a ticket, Jake."

Of course. Piece of cake, like he said. I gave the ticket to Sarah to look after. The ladybird turned round in its tracks and wondered if going the other way would be better.

By the time we picked up speed and edged our way into the traffic, the ladybird had decided that going upwards might be the answer. Very slowly it crawled up the windscreen – I had to point my nose further and further up to keep track of it.

Cars in the middle lane were rushing past outside us, obviously untroubled by the insect life of the region.

Suddenly there was a scraping noise from somewhere in front of us. One of the cars passing us must have got very close indeed.

"Jake!" my sister screamed.

"What the hell was that?" Mum sat forwards in the back seat.

"I dunno…" I wiped my hair away from my face. I was sweating by now.

The odd thing was, everyone was still moving exactly

as we had been. Like you do in a dream. The other car shot out of sight.

I never saw the ladybird again – it must have taken advantage of the kerfuffle to make good its escape.

And like I said, it was only the wheel hub that looked any different: it now had weird black smears on it. *Oh and maybe a slight buckle; but then you don't actually need wheel hubs, do you?*

My mobile is beeping again. Who's this from? Looks like George – I wonder how he's getting on in Paris with the kids? He said he'd text me.

"Your mum's phone is turned off – is she alright?" *What? What the hell is the man on about? Why shouldn't Mum's phone be off – she's probably in a meeting or something.*

Weird. Everyone's gone mad today.

I'm just going to make myself some more tea when there's the sound of a key in the front door.

"Jake? Are you up?" *What's Mum doing back home? Something's wrong.*

As she comes into the kitchen, I see at once that she's been crying.

"Haven't you heard, Jake? Haven't you had the TV on?"

"No… No, I was listening to Coldplay – that CD Annie gave me. Why, what's the matter?"

"The most dreadful thing has happened…"

She sits down at the kitchen table and I pour her a coffee – and then she tells me. As she talks she stirs her spoon in the cup over and over, though she doesn't take sugar. She says some people have set off bombs inside some underground trains in the middle of London – and one in a bus, she thinks.

"I couldn't stay in work, I had to come home."

I can't believe what I'm hearing.

"Is everyone… Was anyone hurt, Mum?"

"What do you think, Jake? Of course they were bloody hurt! Dozens of people are dead. They've no idea how many yet…"

"But what about the people who set off the bombs? I don't understand – how did they manage to get away?"

"They didn't."

Right. I see now.

"I feel so angry, Jake. How can anyone do this to us?"

We sit in silence for a while, staring at each other.

"Your sister's alright, by the way – I rang her," Mum says at last. "She's in the office, but most of her work colleagues have been held up and they haven't been able to get in. There's absolute chaos all over London – no one can get anywhere."

In the end we decide to go into the living room and put the television on. We watch it together as reporters struggle to piece together the awful story. While we watch, I text Annie up in Gleneagles to let her know we are OK here. We gather from the TV that Tony Blair has already left Gleneagles and flown down to London.

It's nearly two hours before I remember the letter on the hall table – from the car hire people; it seems to belong to another age. But I suppose I'd better show Mum.

"What's this? Hertz?"

She tears it open absentmindedly and glances at it. "Oh, they've taken a couple of hundred Euros off my card for damage to the car – look." She shows me the letter. "I don't need to do anything, they've just taken it."

"Yeah?"

She shrugs. "So what?" she says. "As though it MATTERED, for God's sake. After what's happened to us today, Jake… I feel so angry. I'm sorry, I can't take this car rental business seriously."

She drops the letter from Hertz into the waste-paper basket.

Damage was first published in the Bridge House anthology *On This Day*, 2012

8. The Match

Germany's playing in the semi-finals tonight – it's the World Cup in South Africa, a fun occasion for everyone on a blisteringly hot summer's evening. We are going to the village square to watch the match on a big screen at one of the open-air cafés with our grandchildren over a few glasses of beer. We've got English friends staying with us in our home in Bonn, but luckily Jack's wife says that now that England has been knocked out – beaten in Bloemfontein by us! – they are supporting Germany and would love to come along to watch.

Jack and I go back a long way – nearly sixty years.

I always felt hungry sixty years ago. At home my mother cooked only potatoes, and there was barely enough for me and my older brothers. But I had one decent coat and a battered old suitcase, and that summer the pastor at our church selected me to join a party on an exchange visit to England, where we'd each have to stay alone with a family – my English was going to be sorely tested!

A group of English churches had invited young German boys to come over. Our pastor had tried other places but he had drawn a blank nearer home – no one in the Netherlands or Denmark would touch German youths so soon after the Occupation.

So there I was, terrified, just off the boat train at Waterloo, and shivering in the rain in my thin – but decent – coat and wondering what was coming next.

Jack's father came straight up to me on the platform, a pleasant-faced, direct man, holding out his welcoming hand – and I'll never forget Jack – standing shyly behind his father, his bright, well-fed face looking up at me. He's three years younger than me, and he had thick, blond hair and bright, blue eyes.

These days Jack's hair is grey and his face frankly grizzled – "lived in!" says his wife. We grab a couple of tables and push them together near one of the television screens and settle down to get the drinks in. My wife opens some packets of crisps and looks round for our son and his children. The place is pretty crowded already. I notice several of our neighbours are here, and we wave. There's a busy hum about the square, though nothing like as loud as those strange vuvuzelas on the television. German flags are everywhere.

Jack's mother was waiting for us when Jack and his father brought me home on the local train. She stood at the open front door, an umbrella in her hand: "In case anyone should walk past who was getting wet," they told me – I thought that must be a joke, but you can never be sure with English people. She ushered me in out of the rain, and the first thing she said to me was, "How lovely to meet you, Jurgen! Your coat is wet, dear – quick, take it off. Would you like to borrow one of my husband's jackets? You look cold."

That night Jack's mother cooked a heavenly dinner. First his father went into the back garden to dig the potatoes, and Jack took me out to watch him.

"Dig for victory!" said his father. "That's what we were always told during the war, and I've just carried on. I expect you did the same where you come from…"

It was a long, narrow garden with a lawn stretching down from the house. There were fruit trees at the bottom. His dad dug a fork into the potato patch and began to shovel a few smallish specimens into a bucket.

But I was horrified when he stopped after quite a short time, mopped his brow with his handkerchief and put down his fork. "There, that should be enough for tonight. Jack, take the bucket in to Mum, will you?"

There were not nearly enough potatoes in the bucket for all of us – I didn't know how many were expected at table, but presumably at least four? Or maybe even some guests – I had no idea. There was no way those potatoes would all go round. I bit my lip; *what could I say?* I was desperately hungry, but I didn't want to be rude to these kindly people, so I kept quiet.

I followed Jack into the kitchen, where there was the most wonderful smell coming from the oven.

"What time's dinner, Mum? I'm starving!" said Jack.

"We can eat at quarter to – I'll just get these spuds on and do the veg." She turned to me. "I've done a leg of lamb – I do hope you like lamb, Jurgen?"

I nodded dumbly. Of course! That explained why there weren't going to be tons of potatoes – these good people actually ate *meat* and *vegetables* with their meals! My family back home would never believe me when I told them.

My wife is waving across to the next café – looks like the grandchildren are coming over to meet our visitors. Introductions all round. Jack and his wife have even more grandchildren than we do, and his wife strikes up a conversation with our oldest, who is going to study English as one of his subjects at university next year. "You must come over and stay with us some time," she suggests. Then our youngest declares that he needs an ice-cream, so Jack's wife offers to go and get them for everyone before we can stop her.

The rain had gone by the morning after I arrived with Jack's parents. I was snug in the small, cosy bedroom I'd been given, and after lying awake for a while absorbing the strangeness of it all, I slept soundly because I was so tired. I didn't wake up until Jack's mother came in and drew the curtains.

"Oh. look what a beautiful day it is!" she exclaimed. "I've brought you a cup of tea, Jurgen." She put it down on the bedside table and beamed at me. She had the sort of smile that comes from very deep within a person.

That was the day that Jack decided to teach me to play

cricket – not a game I had any experience of, I hardly need to say. A few of his mates from up the road came over to join in, and between them they tried very hard to explain what you are supposed to do – and why. I thought – and to be honest I still think, sixty years later – that it is the weirdest game I have ever come across. But they were friendly enough boys, even though their English was a bit difficult to follow, and later they took me out for a picnic at an open-air swimming pool nearby.

On Sunday morning I went to church with Jack's family, where I met up with two of the other lads I had travelled over with. One of them was staying on a farm, and he told me he enjoyed learning how to milk cows.

The minister began the service by welcoming us all, and afterwards as we stood outside the church in the sun, several of the congregation came over to talk to us. Jack's mother introduced me. Lots of friendly chat; they asked me about my home and my mother, and how I was settling in with Jack's family.

But I noticed one family walk past without a word, grim-faced, staring straight ahead. It was a couple with two young daughters. Jack – who obviously knew them – made some joking comment to the elder girl, but she frowned and shook her head at him as she hurried past.

"Never mind them," Jack's mother said quickly, moving to stand between me and the retreating family.

"Why, what's the matter?" I asked.

"They didn't think we ought to go inviting Germans into our homes – don't take any notice, Jurgen love."

Ah, the action on television is hotting up – they've finished all the pre-match interviews and move over to the football stadium. The teams are coming out, and as the Germans appear there's a great cheer from all the cafés in the square.

My granddaughter is waving a flag. People are dashing inside to place last minute orders for drinks. Kids are rushing round the square on their bikes – it will not be dark for well over an hour.

The national anthems strike up on the television, but no one here takes any notice – we all carry on chatting. Jack's wife pushes back her chair – she looks as though she thinks we are all going to have to stand up, but no. "Don't worry," I assure her. "We don't take the anthem seriously; it has too many resonances for us."

"Really?" she says.

"We still have the same one that Hitler used," I explain. "So we don't like to make a big thing of it."

When the Spanish anthem is played, Jack leans across and whispers to me, "I rather fancy that the group on the next table are Spanish."

He may well be right – they are a lively group of dark-haired young men and could be Spaniards working over here, or on holiday.

At last, all the preambles over, the match is on. We settle down to watch, but the background noise in the square hardly diminishes.

Jack is enjoying himself. It's good to see him again – it has been at least five years since they last came, though of course we get their Christmas card and news every year. He's retired now, and he's sold the business that he built up – he and his wife used to run a small hotel, but they say they don't miss it; it was very hard work during the season.

I've been over to see them a good many times over the years; I used to work in a company that sent me abroad a lot, and it was often easy to fit in a visit to Jack. We went to his wedding of course, and we've seen his children grow up. One very sad occasion – I went to his mother's funeral twenty years ago. I felt that an important link with my past had finally been broken.

Jack's father had been in the Home Guard during the war, and after I'd been with them a few days I felt brave enough to ask him about what he'd had to do. When there were bombing raids, he had been in charge of getting people into the public shelters.

"Oh, that's all in the past," Jack's mother exclaimed. "We've got to leave all that behind us. Now put the kettle on, Jack – who's for another cup of tea?" I could see she felt uncomfortable talking about bombing raids in front of me.

But we'd had bombing raids too.

When I was eight, I was absolutely petrified when my mother took us to Hamburg to stay with an aunt. We all hid together under a great wooden table in the kitchen while the bombs dropped. The whole house shook, and I was sure it would all come crashing down on us. It seemed to me that it went on for many hours. I wanted to go off to have a pee, but my mum wouldn't let me. When at last it was all over, I couldn't stop shaking. I couldn't even speak.

I met many people on my first visit to Jack's family. *I wonder* – now I come to think of it – *what happened to some of them?* There was one old man, a near neighbour of theirs – *do you know, I can't even remember his name* – who talked to me about the war one day, when I ran into him in the street. I happened to be alone, on my way down to meet Jack at the recreation ground. This old man said that he himself had fought in the First World War, and his son had been in the Royal Air Force in the recent war.

"He was a fighter pilot," he said, and I could hear the pride in his voice. "Flew a spitfire." He glared up at me, as

90

though challenging me to deny the worth of the great planes.

"Oh, yes?" I said politely.

"Shot down on his last mission."

There was a small pause before I spoke.

"I'm so sorry." I meant it, too.

"I suppose you were too young. But what about your father, young man? What did he do in the war, eh?" I don't know what answer he expected – did he think my dad might have been a top SS general? Or the Commandant of some frightful camp? But Dad wasn't anything like that – just a humble private. He'd been a baker before the war.

"He was sent to the Russian front," I said. "He died."

"Ah. I see." He shifted his weight on his walking stick. "You'll know, then." He patted my arm. "Good to talk to you, sonny." I noticed that his eyes were glistening as he turned away.

There's gathering tension and loud cheering – looks like Germany is moving towards the goal. Someone makes a brilliant pass – I can't tell who – Jack and I leap out of our seats – we are surely going to score – but no! The ball hits the crossbar and goes astray. Jack crashes his fist down on the table in frustration.

"Damn!" says Jack's wife. "Well, I think I'd better go and get a top up – anyone else?"

"Yes please," we all say – and she takes our orders.

The Spanish boys on the next table are getting pretty excited, and just as Jack's wife arrives with a tray of beers there's an enormous shout of triumph from them – Spain has scored!

That's it, then; there are no more attempts at goal. So it's one-nil at full time, and we are actually out of the World Cup. We will not be in the final. I can't believe it.

My wife is gathering up the grandchildren and telling them we will see them again at the weekend. Our son comes to our table to fetch them. "What a disappointment!" he says. "I really thought we were going to win…"

"Oh well," says Jack's wife. "Never mind. But we do sympathise – we English are pretty used to losing in the World Cup – especially when there's a matter of penalties against you! Jack and I have had a lovely evening, anyway – thank you so much."

And she's right of course: we have all had a lovely evening. And there will be many more, that's for sure.

We are lifelong friends.

9. The End of the Road

Aisling was sick on the boat over to Skellig Michael, poor dab. Mostly over the side – into the choppy waves – only a tiny bit down my coat, and anyway I'm used to my clothes smelling of vomit.

Her mother was furious. "Oh, for heaven's sake, child!" Siobhan roared at her.

Tears welled up in Aisling's eyes as I mopped her up with the cloth I carry in my bag. "Sorry, Gran!" she muttered.

"Cheer up, my love – we're nearly there," I told her. "You'll feel better when we dock." I put my arm around her and squeezed hard. "Clever girl! You're doing fine." She's only six, and she's a stout soul, but someone has to tell her she's OK.

My son took no notice at all – he was in the middle of a flaming row with Siobhan and David wasn't going to be diverted because he generally knows he's right. I couldn't make out exactly what they were arguing about this time; I was too busy making sure Ruaridh didn't hurl himself off the boat while stretching up to look at the amazing white birds which surrounded Little Skellig. Gannets, the guide told us, and Ruaridh was fascinated.

I think the latest row must have been about David's business enterprise. It had been going badly; he'd lost a lot of money on a dodgy deal, which he hadn't wanted to tell me about. He was always like that as a boy – he would never let on if he was in any sort of trouble. Once he got kicked out of the swimming class for chattering too much to his friend, but it was five weeks before I found out.

At last the captain managed to bring our boat into the little harbour which nestled at the foot of this sheer cliff. The guide told us it was seven hundred feet straight up, and I could believe that. Imagine anyone coming here for the first time, all those centuries ago! A tiny, inhospitable offshore island – and yet the community they founded lasted six hundred years.

The guide turned to Aisling. "Perhaps the little girl should get off first," he said kindly, in his soft Irish accent.

The rest of the party turned to look at us sympathetically, and stood back to let us past. I clutched Ruaridh's hand very firmly indeed, thinking "Boy-Over-Board" would not go down well with Siobhan, or indeed with Boy. Aisling managed to jump onto the dry land.

"Good girl!" I said with a cheerful grin. She's always been an anxious child, never sure that she's doing the right thing. A little encouragement from her mother wouldn't come amiss, I'd often thought over the years, but Siobhan is a hard, brittle person who hasn't much time for small children. You know, this is odd, given that she is a consultant child psychiatrist, one of the best ever to come out of Dublin they tell me, but there you go.

When we'd all disembarked, we had to climb the steep,

narrow steps up to the top. I knew Aisling would make it, given time and holding my hand tight, but I persuaded David that little Ruaridh needed a lift.

"Right then, here we go!" David hoisted his son onto his broad shoulders. He seemed relieved to be distracted from the row with Siobhan. He concentrated on climbing up carefully, while telling the children how the early Irish monks had first arrived here and built their monastery and their little beehive-shaped stone huts. He walked in front of us, while Siobhan dropped behind, getting into conversation with a young couple in the party who were clearly more interesting than us.

Siobhan gets so impatient with me whenever there are any steps to climb up. I can do steps, you understand, it's just that I take a lot longer over them than I used to, and puff a lot as I go along.

Aisling cheered up as we climbed, and began to look around.

"Do people live here now, Gran?" she asked.

"Oh no, not for many years, darling. It's just the birds now! The monks left long ago. But there used to be a lighthouse keeper living here with his family, you know. You'll see the lighthouse when we get to the top – it's still there – to warn the ships not to come too near."

David turned round and added, "The lighthouse is solar powered these days – do you know what that means, Aisling?"

I was quite out of breath when we finally reached the top, and David pointed to a bench that some kind person had put there. I must admit that the view was amazing. "Come and sit with me, Aisling," I said, not wanting to let her run around on her own. We could see right across to the inner island, Little Skellig, which looked white because of all those thousands of birds perched on it or flying around it. I'd never seen so many birds before.

"Look out there," David said, pointing the other way, across the Atlantic. "There's nothing there at all except ocean, until you get to – do you know where, Aisling?"

Aisling looked uncertain.

"Oh, you might as well tell her, David," Siobhan snapped, coming over and standing by the bench. "Daddy wants to go and work in America, don't you? Not content with running the business into the ground in Cardiff, your father thinks he can make a new start in the USA and in no time at all become a millionaire! What do you think of that, children?"

I was suddenly aware of the cold wind howling round the little bench, and I put out my hand on the wooden arm to steady myself.

"It's all right, Mum!" David said at once. "Don't panic. Nothing's decided. It was just an idea that a colleague of mine in New York floated past me."

Just an idea. I see. Not something David would have thought of mentioning if Siobhan hadn't brought it up.

"Can I have an ice-cream, Gran?" Ruaridh was jumping up and down now and tugging at my bag.

David laughed. "Not here, you can't, Ruaridh! Can you see the ice-cream van? Where do you think it is, behind that cliff over there? Or in the ruined monastery?"

Luckily, I'd got some popcorn in my bag, and I got it out. I dished it out rather cautiously, thinking we shouldn't fill Aisling up with too much junk – there was always the return boat trip to contemplate. Siobhan disappeared – she must have needed a smoke.

By this time I was beginning to get my breath back after the steep climb, and I stood up. There was a wonderful fresh smell of the sea, and I felt quite energetic as I took each child by the hand and suggested that we explore a bit. We found a beehive hut near the edge of a cliff and paused to look at it.

"Why is it called beehive, Gran?" Aisling asked.

"It must be the shape, I suppose. Imagine making it out of stone – those monks didn't have all the building materials we use nowadays – just what they could find lying around on the island."

"Mind you hang onto those children, madam!" The guide came up behind us. "There's a sheer drop just here."

"Oh goodness yes!" I said.

"Did any of the monks ever fall down?" Aisling asked the man.

He paused to consider; he was one of those people who really listen to children and try to answer their questions. "I don't think we know that – maybe they did. It's quite likely. But I'll tell you what we do know, young lady…"

"What?"

"You see that lighthouse across there?" He pointed to it as it stood out on another ridge of the island. "Nobody lives there now, it just works all on its own, but until about twenty-five years ago there used to be a lighthouse keeper living there."

What an isolated place to live!

"He lived alone," the guide went on. "But in the century before that, the lighthouse keeper lived here with all his family, children and all. There was one lighthouse keeper called William Callaghan who had little ones – about your age, they were."

Even Ruaridh was listening with interest by now.

"One December day his younger son Patrick was playing out on the rocks, and he slipped and fell off the cliff. He was only two – how old are you – young man?"

"Four!" said Ruaridh proudly.

"Well, I'm afraid young Patrick was killed when he hit the rocks down there." He paused for the shock of this to sink in, then he went on, "But what do you think happened

97

only three months later? His big brother William, who was four like you, he went and fell down the same rocks and he was killed too."

I held the children's hands a little tighter. "When was this?" I asked, when I was able to speak.

"Oh, it was back in 1868, and March '69. The children are buried in the graveyard of the medieval chapel. William Callaghan wrote a letter to Head Office explaining what had happened and respectfully begging to be moved to a different job. He'd come to the end of the road, poor man. We still have the letter, in beautiful copperplate handwriting."

After a moment's silence, I suggested that we should walk back up, away from the cliff.

Aisling was fine on the boat back, but I still kept hold of her. David thinks I'm a bit of a clucky old hen, but then you see I'd practically brought these children up. I lived in the next street to them in Cardiff, and Siobhan couldn't wait to hand them over to me as soon as she'd given birth. Fair play, she had severe depression after Aisling was born – which explains a lot about her feelings for the girl – I've always thought; I never once heard her give the child any sort of praise. Her doctor said she ought to return to work as soon as possible in order to recover. They could have sent the baby to a crèche, but money was tight and I was only too willing to take over. Siobhan worked long hours at the hospital, and she would often come home after I'd put Aisling to bed. As for David, he was very often away on business trips. Somehow, we slipped into the same pattern when Ruaridh arrived, and I used to take Aisling to school.

Back on Valentia Island – dry land! We stopped off briefly at a café and then made our way to the hire car. The children and I snuggled down on the back seat, and pretty soon they were both asleep, worn out by the fresh air and excitement of the day. Ruaridh lay diagonally right across me, breathing deeply, his face flushed, the pattern of my coat etched on his cheek. Aisling rested her head on my shoulder.

We'd booked into a hotel in Dingle, so we had to go round to the far end of the bay. I was alarmed to see that Siobhan was going to drive; not that she isn't an excellent driver – she's a perfectionist and she drives as she does everything else – getting it right by the book. (You know she must be a marvellous psychiatrist.) But the trouble is that my son cannot resist instructing her.

It begins with little things. "You do realise they drive on the left here, just like in Cardiff?"

Wisely Siobhan ignores this.

Then we get slowed down by a couple of large lorries on the N70 before we get to Killorglin. "I think you might overtake this lot – we want to get to the hotel before midnight," David says mildly. This is his pretend mild tone.

Siobhan continues steadily behind the lorries.

"It's perfectly safe, I tell you," David goes on, raising his voice ever so slightly.

"David," she says with icy calm, "just shut the fuck up, will you?"

He is quiet for a minute, then as it looks as though we are coming to a straight bit of road Siobhan suddenly swerves and comes out from behind the first lorry.

Oh my God! There's a car coming straight towards us. Fast.

I close my eyes.

"What the hell are you doing, woman?" David shouts. I think he actually grabs the wheel, and she – well, one of them, at any rate – just manages to get back in behind the lorry.

We go along in silence for quite a way, then. David

wipes his forehead on his sleeve and pushes back his hair in an exaggerated gesture. Siobhan stares grimly ahead.

"You OK in the back there?" David says, glancing round after a moment.

"Oh yes – absolutely. Never better." Irony has always been one of my strong points.

After checking in at the hotel, we walked down to the harbour in the cool of the evening. David and I stood alone by the shore: a peaceful, busy scene; hundreds of boats, big and small. Advertisements for boat trips – sea angling, Blasket Island, Fungie the dolphin – the children might like that, I point out to David, but I gather there are rumours that Fungie is dead. As it turned out, he wasn't, but it fitted my mood.

"Look Mum, there's something I've been meaning to tell you," David says.

Instantly I forget all about Fungie, dead or alive.

I take a deep breath. "Yes?"

"Siobhan's been headhunted. She's been offered a job in a big hospital in Edinburgh."

Steady, now. "Really? Is she going to take it?"

"She hasn't decided yet. At least, I don't think she has. But she's tempted. It would be a big step up – she'd be head of her own unit. Able to do things she's always wanted to do."

I am beginning to feel quite dizzy. "Yes, I see. Edinburgh, you say?"

There are thick black clouds gathering over the hills above Dingle, and they seem to match everything else about the day.

The children went off to sleep quickly that night, but I couldn't sleep for some time. I kept thinking what would happen if Siobhan took the job in Edinburgh. *What would*

I do? Would David expect me to move up there with them?

I heard David and Siobhan talking in the next room for what seemed like hours through the night. They were not too loud most of the time, but occasionally voices were raised in anger. I couldn't hear what they were saying.

Next morning it was pouring with rain, and the waiter in the hotel was quick to offer a suggestion. As he brought us plates of scrambled egg and smoked salmon for breakfast, he said the children might like the Oceanworld Aquarium.

"Oh, thank you," I said. "What a good idea!"

"Yes, Mum," David said, "but how would it be if you took them there on your own this morning? I'm afraid we didn't have too good a night – Siobhan needs a rest."

To be honest, I'd never seen Siobhan look so terrible. Her hair was tangled, which was most unlike her, and her face white as chalk except for the dark rings under her eyes. She hadn't put on her makeup, and she had hardly spoken a word at breakfast. David himself didn't look good either. There was a wildness in his eyes, and he hadn't noticed when Aisling asked him for some orange juice.

"Oh dear – I am sorry," I said. "I hope you manage to get some rest, dear…" But Siobhan wasn't listening.

As quickly as I could, I got the children away and took them down to the aquarium by the shore.

We loved the penguins of course, but the best part – we all agreed – was a big installation called a Touch Tank. It was an open stretch of water with lots of creatures swimming around it, and if you were tall enough you could lean over the edge and actually stroke the fish in the water as they went past. I had to lift Ruaridh up and hold him tight round the waist while he stroked a ray as it flapped along. Aisling was nervous at first, but she soon

101

got the idea, and she was delighted to find a starfish that let her hold it.

"This is the best day of my whole life!" Aisling said as the three of us sat in a damp café having fish and chips for lunch.

There was a stunned silence when David finished speaking. We had all gathered in the children's bedroom in the hotel, and he had explained that he was taking up the chance to go to New York and expand his business – just for a few months, a year perhaps – and give Siobhan the chance to take up her amazing new post.

"I don't understand," Aisling said at last. "How will I get to school?"

Siobhan sighed impatiently. "You don't have to go to *that* crappy school, you stupid child – you'll go to a new one, a much better one, in Edinburgh. Lucky girl, you'll have wonderful new friends!"

Aisling stared at her mother as if she must be the stupid one. "But Gran takes me to school every day. How will she get there?"

David looked out of the window and fiddled with his pen.

Evidently David wasn't going to be part of this amazing new life in Edinburgh. Siobhan was taking the children away from him; they had come to the end of the road. What was more, it was quite clear to me that I wasn't going to be wanted any more either – Siobhan would be glad to see the last of me.

I cleared my throat. "I'm afraid I won't be able to come with you when you move, Aisling. I'm so sorry." I was floundering now, but I went on, "You're just going to have to be a really big girl... and remember all the things I've told you about how clever you are... And there'll be so many exciting new things to do, I'm sure."

102

"Oh for God's sake don't you start crying!" Siobhan turned on me in fury. "You'll set the children off, you silly old woman."

But it was too late; it seemed I already had.

10. All in a Day's Work

From the Manager
Tesco Express, Ty Gwyn Avenue

Dear Mrs Blenkinsop,

Thank you for your letter of 31st August. I regret that as we are a relatively small store we do not have the space for a Christmas Grotto along the lines that you suggest, and so I must decline your kind offer to act as Mother Christmas in December.

Thank you for your complimentary remarks about our store, and I hope that you will continue to shop with us.

Yours sincerely,

J. S. Dobbs (Manager)

Dear Mrs Blenkinsop,

Thank you for your further letter of 5th September. As I said last week, we are not a large store and so we would struggle to find space for a Witches' Coven along the lines you suggest. I'm afraid it would not be feasible to replace the entire World Food Ready Meals aisle for the last fortnight of October as you recommend, as they are a very popular product.

Therefore we will not be able to employ you as an In-store Witch at Halloween.

However, it was an ingenious suggestion, and I am glad to see that you are a regular shopper with us.

Yours sincerely,
J. S. Dobbs (Manager)

Dear Mrs Blenkinsop,

Thank you for your further letter of 10th September. No, I must confess that I had not heard the rumour that pumpkins are likely to be much smaller this year. This may well be a late silly-season scare story, and to be perfectly frank I find it hard to believe. I must assure you that all our pumpkins are of the highest quality and locally sourced, so we will not be needing to avail ourselves of your kind offer to supply us with extra-large ones...

Yours sincerely,
J. S. Dobbs (Manager)

Dear Mrs Blenkinsop,

I must protest in the strongest possible terms at your further letter of 16th September. I assure you that I was NOT aware that your partner was of mixed Ghanaian and Jewish extraction, and I strongly refute the implication that if I had known this, it would have influenced my decision as to whether to employ you as a witch in our store, or indeed to purchase giant pumpkins from your allotment. Such decisions are generally left to me as manager, and I can assure you they are NEVER affected by considerations of race; my wife is in fact Chinese, as it happens.

As I explained, we simply do not have the room for a grotto of any sort, nor do I feel that it would add to our appeal as a family convenience store. Some of the illustrations you sent would, I feel, be downright terrifying to small children. My own daughter is just four, and when I showed your picture to her, she burst into tears and declared that she would not be coming to Daddy's work anymore in the future.

Yours sincerely,

J. S. Dobbs (Manager)

Dear Mrs Blenkinsop,

As I thought I had made clear in my letter last week, I have absolutely no prejudice against any race, let alone the Jews or Black people in general, nor, indeed, any other race. I deeply resent your accusation and I find it inexplicable that you have resorted to a solicitor to deal with this matter. Since we have never agreed to employ you, there cannot possibly be any question of unfair dismissal and you have no rights under employment legislation. I'm sure that your solicitor will advise you of this...

Yours sincerely,

J. S. Dobbs (Manager)

Dear Mrs Blenkinsop,

I have been informed by our national Head Office that I should not engage further in correspondence with you, since you have placed my letters in the hands of your solicitor.

I would, however, just like to add that when you referred to your partner, I had absolutely no idea that yours is a civil partnership and that she is in fact a woman. You are quite wrong in inferring that I must have read about your ceremony in the South Wales Echo. I assure you that those articles passed me by. My work as Manager here is extremely stressful and takes up pretty well every waking moment of my life – my wife keeps a photo of me in her purse to remind her what I look like – and I simply do not have time to read idle tittle-tattle in the newspapers.

I must assure you that I am in no way prejudiced against same-sex partnerships.

Yours indignantly

J.S. Dobbs (Manager)

Dear Mrs Blenkinsop,

As I thought I had informed you on 1st October, our Chief Executive in Welwyn Garden City has personally intervened and forbidden me from corresponding with you. Indeed my GP has warned me that to continue to do so could seriously harm my health.

However, I would just like to object in the strongest possible terms to the assortment of parcels that you have been bombarding my store with this week. I thought I had made it clear that we do not require any large pumpkins as we have a perfectly adequate supply from our loyal, local producers. Would you kindly arrange to have your goods removed as they are taking up nearly all the space in our storeroom, please? THIS IS A MATTER OF URGENCY.

Furthermore, we do not have any use for the masks and other stuff – I am tempted to use the word "rubbish" – that you have sent us. We did not ask for any of this. I appreciate that you and your partner made all the items by hand, using recycled materials and without taking up scarce energy resources or harming the environment in any way; that is of course admirable, but we cannot accept your items as we have our own Halloween supplies which are due to arrive this Thursday. You must therefore arrange to have your parcels collected as soon as possible.

Yours sincerely,
J. S. Dobbs (Manager)

1st November

Dear Mrs Blenkinsop,

Your appearance in my store yesterday was completely unacceptable.

The noise of a dozen small children recruited from Ton-yr-Ywen primary school singing, or perhaps I should say shouting, songs involving what appeared to be some sort of devil worship was shocking in the extreme. Mrs Timms, who is a very regular customer of ours, had to be taken to Casualty after two of them knocked her stick away when she refused their demand of "trick or treat". I understand this morning that although doctors kept her in overnight as a precaution, she is expected to make a good recovery and will not after all need surgery; you will no doubt be glad to learn this.

You and your partner were dressed in the most grotesque costumes, as you must be well aware. I hardly feel that long fangs were appropriate when thrust into the faces of several of our more elderly customers who happen to have false teeth.

It was quite unacceptable of you to strip bare the whole aisle devoted to our ready-made sandwiches and install your own products there. As I tried to protest at the time, we do not wish to market your toffee apples, wholesome though you claim them to be, nor indeed are we able to sell products containing snails or parts of toads.

When the police cleared the store, I fear that we lost a significant number of long-standing and valued customers, many of whom were heard to mutter as they left that they were off to Sainsbury's. I hold you personally responsible for this outcome.

I should respectfully like to inform you that I shall not be answering your letters in future, should you wish to communicate further, as I have been placed on indefinite sick leave. My deputy Mr T. Roberts will take over as Acting Manager until a replacement can be appointed.

Yours very sincerely,
James St. John Dobbs
(Former Manager)

11. Celebration

For some reason my Quaker Meeting decided to make a big thing out of my ninetieth birthday. An outdoor party, they said, as it would be May – with lots of food, and naturally a cake. Brenda volunteered to make it; she would, of course. Brenda can always be relied upon to get involved, whether appropriately or not. No, that's not fair; I made a resolution last January not to be nasty about Brenda; I can safely leave that to the younger ones.

"We thought we'd have it at my place, if you wouldn't mind too much, Charlotte?" Ursula peered at me anxiously through her thick, pebble glasses, as she balanced a mug of tea on her knee.

I laughed. "That sounds superb, Ursula dear – why on earth should I mind?"

Ursula ran the local library and lived alone in a large, detached house with a rambling garden. Her husband had been killed in a car crash about ten years before, and her youngest child was away at university by now. I love Ursula's garden, and it struck me that if we were lucky her glorious rhododendron bushes would be out in time.

"We were afraid you might want to have it at the Meeting House," Ursula went on. "As it falls on a Sunday?"

"No, not specially. Have some more cake, Ursula?"

She leant across and took another slice. "In that case, Ian wondered if you'd mind if he did a barbecue? His son gave him a kit for Christmas and he tries it out at the drop of a hat…"

"What fun!" I cried. "We could get some steaks and lots of sausages. And chicken legs. Oh, and we'd have to have plenty of vegetarian stuff. Those veggie burgers can be quite tasty. In their way…"

There was more to it than the food, of course. Someone – Ian, I think – it would be so like Ian – had had the bright idea of doing a sort of "This Is Your Life" for me. I don't know what dark secrets they thought they were going to unearth, mind. Bankruptcy, drug addiction, a succession of lovers, unsubstantiated allegations that I'd once been a member of the Conservative Party, that sort of thing… No, he probably had in mind old photographs and keepsakes.

I like Ian. He's a social worker, rather a short man, with a thick, greying beard. I suppose he was in his early forties by then, worked off his feet of course; why is it that everyone nowadays seems to be either unemployed or have far too much work to do? Ian lived alone just across St Peter's Close from my own sheltered flat; he used to call in now and then, late at night. He was lonely, I think.

When Ursula had gone, I decided to look out some of my old photograph albums in case they were required for this occasion that the Meeting apparently wanted. I'd kept all my albums when I moved out of our home after Arnold died, even though my daughter Margaret had tut-tutted a good deal and sniffed and said that surely I wouldn't have room for all that junk in the new, little flat?

I kept Arnold's battered old trunk that he'd had in China during the War; it fitted snugly into the corner of my tiny spare room, and in it I stored my letters and photographs. Down at the bottom were the oldest – my mother's record of our childhood. Not personal pictures from our home of course – my parents never possessed a camera – but whenever one of us reached some significant landmark in life we were hauled down to the photographer in the High Street for an official portrait among the aspidistras. There was rather a charming one of me, aged about six. I was wearing a longish, white dress with puffed sleeves and a locket round my neck. My fluffy, fair hair was held up in a bow, and I stood solemnly between my parents; not one of us smiling. My father's handlebar moustache was trim; he sat sideways on an armchair, facing the camera with his bald head apparent. My mother sat bolt upright, her long, dark dress fastened at the neck with a velvet bow, her hands clasped decorously in her lap. *The sheer determination in the set of that chin; how often had I observed it in Margaret!*

I remember that day. I'd been sick twice that very morning and there was some doubt about whether they could bring me after all, but the photographer had been booked at great expense and my mother was loathe to waste the money. The man took forever arranging the chairs, and I was wondering what would be the polite thing to say – and do – if I felt sick again, an eventuality which seemed to grow ever more likely the more I dwelt on it.

The next photograph showed our whole family, taken perhaps a year or so later. My parents were seated next to each other in the garden with me standing just behind them, peering over their shoulders. On either side of them stood their only two surviving sons, for a number of babies and young children had died in the years before my own birth. Tom and Freddie looked almost grownup in that picture. *Ah yes, Freddie was wearing an academic gown. It must have been the year he went up to Oxford.*

I leafed through a few more pages – a number of cousins – most of whom lived near us, and a few picture postcards. Then the last page, a single photograph on its own: Tom in the uniform of an army officer. He stood tall and upright, unblinking – as though he knew the photographer was going to make a sudden flash and he was determined not to react. Tom was just eighteen.

I took the photograph album into the sitting room and found a space for it on the bookcase. Then on impulse I decided to ring my old friend Oliver; as it happens he is also my solicitor, but this wasn't official.

"Have you heard about this 'do' they're having for my birthday?" I demanded. "I suppose it was your idea, was it?"

He chuckled – I love the deep, fruity way he does that on the phone. "Oh, it was one of those ideas that seem to strike lots of people all at the same moment. I suppose it may have been me who first mentioned your greatly advanced age and indeed your impending anniversary… Solicitors are supposed to know things like that, you know."

I snorted.

"And straight away Brenda said we couldn't possibly let such an occasion pass unmarked. You know what Brenda is like."

"I'm afraid I do."

"And Gerry said he could bring along his homemade elderflower wine, so long as we didn't hold it at the Meeting House of course."

"Ah that was it. Would he bring his wife, do you think? I haven't seen Bel for over a year." I rather liked Gerry's wife.

"Gerry said she might just possibly come," Oliver told me. "But she doesn't want a fuss made about her sudden reappearance!"

"I'm not sure what anyone can do to prevent that," I said. "Anyhow, I can leave someone else to sort that out. Tell you what, Olly – why don't you turn up as Olive?"

There was a pause.

Just long enough for me to wonder if I'd put my foot in it.

"I doubt if that would be a terribly good idea, Charlotte love," he said at last.

"Why not? Don't you think it's about time that Olive made our general acquaintance? She's had enough of quiet soirees at St Peter's Close. Ian agrees with me – it's time Olive branched out a bit. Now let me see – how about that lovely lemon-yellow gingham dress? Really summery – perfect for a barbecue, you know."

He laughed. "I'm not sure that the Meeting is ready for Olive yet, my dear. I'll think about it…"

The very next day a postcard arrived from the Great Wall of China. I put on my glasses and peered at the picture – you know – the familiar one of the ancient highway weaving its way up and down the steep mountains which stretched endlessly into the distance. *I'm sure Arnold never went there when he was in China. Is it really true you can see it from the moon?*

The card was from Jenny of course. My granddaughter Jenny, the youngest by a long way, and the only one who lived round the corner from Arnold and me when she was little. I turned the card over and read it. "Hi, Gran! Arrived safe from Cairns last Friday. Got taught how to snorkel on the Great Barrier Reef by a huge hunk of an Ozzie – you must try it some time. China is amazing! Have been cycling all round Beijing. I'm with some people who want to try and get to India, but I'll be back long before your birthday, promise. Lots of love and blackcurrant jam on toast, Jenny."

I smiled and began to clear a space on my kitchen notice board – that list of coffee mornings at St Peter's Retirement Flats could go in the bin and so indeed could "Your Cholesterol Lowering Diet Plan" that my daughter Margaret had put up for me. I pinned the Great Wall of China in the centre and stood back. I really ought to phone Margaret – she and Walter had been getting a little anxious about Jenny a week or so back, but maybe they too had had a card this morning.

Dear Jenny. How was she? She sounded almost her old self.

Jenny used to work in her father Walter's stationery firm, in fact in another year or two he had planned to make her a partner. Well, it was better than being involved in the arms trade, I suppose. The business was thriving – people would always need paperclips, Margaret said – and you couldn't argue with that; but I did wonder if there wasn't something which one could sell that was in between paperclips and spare parts for land mines. *Oh, I don't know, books for instance, or theatre tickets, or trips in hot air balloons, or vodka.*

Jenny's marriage at only twenty had come as a great surprise to me. I'd known the young man for years – he was destined to be Walter's junior partner in the firm – a solid, reliable kind of fellow, not bad looking if you liked that type. Margaret liked him a lot, I could tell. They had a big wedding at Margaret's church – reception at the town's most expensive hotel – the works. I was photographed at the lychgate as the "Grandmother of the Bride". I overheard someone muttering that I was "marvellous for my age", which does irritate me so. And ever worse – someone else muttered that I certainly still had all my marbles. I felt like telling them my hearing wasn't that bad, either.

Jenny left him eight and a half months later.

I put her up in my spare room and shared a good few bars of chocolate with her while I let her cry. We sat up late every night and talked about lever-arch files and ball-point pens, Penelope Lively and Joanna Trollope; about Arnold's absence in China when our children were little and his curious absence now from St Peter's Close; and about the Victoria Falls and the Grand Canyon – and Adelaide – where two of Jenny's closest school friends had recently gone to work.

It was I who gave Jenny the money to go out to Adelaide on an open-ended visit.

Naturally Margaret was furious with me.

"How *dare* you interfere, Mother?" she demanded. "The child's behaved abominably – to all the rest of us – let alone her wretched husband! Who is distraught, incidentally, not that you would care… And as for her poor father, Walter can't even bring himself to talk about her."

I did care about Jenny's husband, as it happened, but I could see that Margaret was not going to credit that. I couldn't help remembering something that my old friend Harold Loukes wrote – oh, more than thirty years ago when he and Arnold were working on some committee together – but I'm gratified to see his words still appear years after his death; I was glancing at that new red book only the other day. Harold talked about the breakdown of marriage, and the need to support those to whom it happens. He said that if we can't do that – it would be like saying that letting someone down within a marriage was an especially unforgivable sin – whereas we know that in reality it is hard to avoid, unlike robbing a bank, which is easier to avoid and more open to forgiveness... That appealed to me.

But Margaret was not impressed. "Really Mother I wonder about you sometimes! What the *hell* has robbing a bank got to do with this sorry mess that young Jenny has got us all into?"

The day I got the Great Wall postcard, I rang Margaret after lunch. It turned out that she and Walter had not heard from Jenny for a couple of months now.

"Nice of you to let us know," Margaret said icily. "Poor Walter was beginning to wonder if she'd set off for a short walk to Ayers Rock."

"Isn't it great that she'll be back for my birthday," I went on, ignoring her tone. "By the way, there's some news about that – you'll never guess what the Meeting is planning to do..."

I told her.

Margaret said that in that case, if the Sunday was booked, I'd better come out to dinner with the family on the Saturday night, which sounded fine to me. She'd get in touch with her brothers and their wives and all their numerous offspring. "And I hope you're behaving yourself these days, Mother," she went on.

"I can't think what you mean!"

You see I'd had a check-up at the doctor's a few months

117

ago, and they were so pleased with me that I was walking particularly cheerfully over the world afterwards, and ended up at my favourite fish shop. As the assistant – who looked vaguely familiar – was weighing out some prawns in their shells for me, I had a sudden, dreadful thought: I'd been so anxious about the check-up that I'd come out without my purse.

"I know you, don't I?" I said.

"Marmalade," he smiled. "I've seen you in Meeting – you're Charlotte, aren't you?" He had long, dark hair tied back in a ponytail and was wearing a white coat which disguised how absurdly thin he was. I'm afraid it took me a moment to recall that Marmalade was in fact his name – a friend of mine in Watford Meeting had written to our Clerk to ask her to look out for a shy young Friend called Marmalade who was moving to our area.

I explained with some embarrassment that I'd forgotten my money, but Marmalade just said he'd pay for the prawns himself until he saw me again. He recommended the skate too, and I went home with a nice wing for my tea.

I really shouldn't have told Margaret this story.

After my phone call to Margaret, I went into the kitchen and put the kettle on. *Marmalade, now; I hadn't thought about him for a month or two – had he been in Meeting?* I knew Ursula was worried about him; he didn't know many people, and he lived alone in a rather dismal bed-sit near the station with a small pet snake called Rupert. *Perhaps I should ring him that evening?*

I glanced at the calendar which I keep pinned up next to my favourite poem. Jenny had copied it out for me in beautiful handwriting a year or so ago when she was doing calligraphy in an evening class. The poem is called *Warning* – I don't know if you know it? It's by another Jenny, Jenny Joseph.

When I am an old woman I shall wear purple
With a red hat which doesn't go and doesn't suit me
And I shall spend my pension on brandy...

Jenny – *my* Jenny that is – said the poem reminded her of me because of the bit about sitting down on the pavement when I'm tired, and gobbling up samples in shops, and pressing alarm bells. She could just see me doing that; not a bit of it, I protested, although I did wonder if running my stick along public railings might be rather fun. But I don't want to learn to spit, and I certainly wouldn't pick flowers in other people's gardens.

Marmalade was delighted when I rang that evening. He wasn't busy – he was about to go out alone and buy himself a Chinese takeaway – so I suggested he should let me treat him and bring two portions round to my flat to share together.

"Ursula tells me you have a pet snake," I said as I popped the beef chop suey and egg fried rice into the microwave.

"Yes, that's right – Rupert." A look of what I can only describe as serenity came over his face. "He's only five months old."

"That must be... er... interesting. I suppose you don't have to exercise him – not like having to take a dog for a walk!" I rather hoped that he didn't take Rupert out at all.

"I have to keep him in a tank at seventy degrees all the time, which gets quite expensive. He's very affectionate," Marmalade went on. "His skin is quite smooth to handle, you know. People are surprised; they expect it to feel scaly."

"Yes, I see." Frankly I wished afterwards that I hadn't asked him next what he fed his snake on.

"Mice, mainly. I have to get them at the market – they're cheap at the moment."

119

"Really – how fascinating." I swallowed, and changed the subject. "By the way, have you heard about this party the Meeting is having for my birthday?"

He had indeed. He and Ian had apparently been planning a free-standing display screen which Ian intended to borrow from the Social Work department, and they were wondering what they could put on it. After we'd eaten, I took him into the living room and showed him my photograph album.

"So did you come from a military family, Charlotte?" he asked as he settled back comfortably on the sofa to listen.

I told him that my father – one of the gentlest people I've ever known – was in fact a bowler-hatted civilian official in the War Office who worked in Aldershot. After I was born we lived on the main road to Frensham Common, where the army held its manoeuvres – sham fights, we called them. Our family was brought up to believe that the Royal Army was an institution to be justly proud of. I remember as a little girl getting terribly excited when the soldiers came galloping down the hill outside our front gate, trailing their guns behind them. My cousins and I would sit on the gatepost to watch them, and we'd cheer like mad as they passed by. Nearly all my cousins were boys, and sometimes if my mother wasn't looking I'd sneak off with them onto Frensham Common and play in the heather when an army exercise was planned.

"An exciting thing happened to my brother Tom once, on Frensham Common," I told Marmalade.

"The one in the photo?"

"That's right, but long before that photo, when he was only a child. He was hiding in the heather one day when the army was out on the common and he saw a small cavalcade of horsemen coming. Suddenly this huge great horse jumped right over him. The rider had no idea there was a boy hiding there, but afterwards father told us that it had been none other than the King, that is Edward VII."

"Wow! That would be before the First World War, then? Do you remember the war, Charlotte?"

"I should say so," I told him. "I was eight when it started. I remember going out for a family walk in the country the day before – our family always did that on August bank holiday – all of us together. It was Monday 3rd August. Father was very quiet; he obviously knew that war was on the cards. Tom and Freddie were preoccupied, too – no one seemed in the mood to play with me. I felt like a little puppy who suddenly finds itself ignored!"

Marmalade laughed and helped both of us to some more cider. "So, your brother Tom joined the army?"

"Oh yes – he was down on the steps of the nearest recruiting office the moment it opened next morning."

"Yes?"

"He'd been in the OTC at school of course – the Officers' Training Corps, you know? So he was made an officer straight away and eventually sent out to France. He was in the second battle of Ypres…"

"What happened to him?" Marmalade lent forward and looked at me.

"In three days he was dead."

"Oh Charlotte, how dreadful!" The young man's eyes filled with tears, and it struck me that he must himself be only three or four years older than my brother Tom had been. I was more touched by Marmalade's tears than I could tell him.

"We never got over it," I said. "No one in the family, really. Tom was everyone's favourite, all his life. We worshipped him."

"What about your other brother – Freddie, was it? What happened to him? If that had been me I'd have been so

121

angry that anyone had killed my brother that I'd want to hit back as hard as I could."

I shrugged. "Yes, a lot of people did feel that. Do you know they even stoned dachshund dogs in the streets because they were German!"

"No!"

"Oh yes, there were lots of stories like that. And I daresay the same thing happened in Germany. But Freddie was quite different from Tom. Quite different."

The phone interrupted us at that moment, and Marmalade stood up, saying he'd really have to be going home because Rupert missed him so much if he was out too long. I waved him off and returned to the phone. It was Oliver, to tell me about a concert at the Town Hall soon. "It's Brahms' First, among other things, and I know that's one of your favourites, Charlotte. Ursula is free, and we're all meeting for a quick pizza beforehand."

That sounded fun. When we'd finished talking, I went back to the kitchen to clear up. *Dear distant Tom.* He suddenly felt very close to me that evening as I stood at the sink washing up. I'd never really known him in life, not in the way siblings can know each other as adults. I'd only been a little girl, and he'd been away at school most of the time. But I remember the excitement in the house when he was due home for the holidays, my mother instructing cook to prepare his favourite meal the first day. I even remember holding my breath – quite literally – when I was lying in bed that night, because my father told me that Tom would not come home at all until I went to sleep like a good girl, and since I couldn't possibly do that I had to pretend. I could never understand why it made my father laugh so, while I quietly went purple in the face.

I enjoyed my flat here at St Peter's, I reflected as I put away the plates in the pine cupboard above the cooker. It was modern and light, well designed with big, wide windows overlooking an interesting street on one side, and a leafy garden on the other. But the strange thing about it was... well, that somehow Arnold wasn't here. Believe me, he was everywhere in our old house, which we'd shared for forty years. Not just obvious places, the living room, the bedroom. He was even in places like the garden shed, where he used to go and sit, reading on a deckchair when visiting grandchildren got too boisterous. Then there was the cupboard under the stairs, a big place that you could walk right into, that Arnold used as a dark room for his photography.

I left all that behind. I knew I had to; people told me it was only sensible now that I was on my own. But it was Oliver, my dear friend, not just the solicitor handling the sale of the house – Olly who warned me that it would make it much harder to begin with. And he was right – I missed Arnold far more in the new flat. *Ah well.*

Like most people, my friend Oliver is a mixture. He is capable of being extraordinarily sensitive over things like my having to sell my home, and if I were ever in serious trouble it is certainly to Oliver that I would turn. He's kind and considerate, and thoughtful, but at the same time he has a life-time's experience in a busy solicitors' practice. He has a fine and penetrating legal mind and he has made his way up the profession by being competitive and often aggressive. But what makes Oliver so odd is that he himself sees these different qualities as belonging to two different personalities. You know the funny old chap actually thinks that it is "Olive" who is sensitive and caring, while "Oliver" is commanding and cutthroat. I suppose that's why he needs to dress the different parts. I don't seem to be able to convince him that we, all of us, are a mixture. At least, that's my view – but I'm sure there's a lot about it that I don't understand.

A few days after Marmalade's visit I went across to see Ian in the evening and found a large map of North America spread out on the floor. He was going to apply for a job in Oregon, he told me.

My heart sank – I'd really miss him. *And perhaps I wouldn't be the only one?*

"Oliver's getting tickets for a concert at the Town Hall, did you know? I think Ursula is coming," I said hopefully.

In fact, I saw Ursula the next morning – I walked over to the library – and Ursula told me that the latest Dick Francis novel had come in and she'd slipped it under the counter for me.

"Oh how kind of you!"

I mentioned Ian swanning off to Oregon, but she looked vague and didn't appear to have heard about it. She was keen to tell me that Brenda was coming in that morning – it was her morning for the flower arranging class upstairs.

Damn. I would have left changing my library books till the afternoon if I'd remembered that.

I heard a clatter of footsteps along the passage and a sudden whoop of delight. "Charlotte! How wonderful – you're looking so much better..." There was no mistaking Brenda's penetrating voice as she came into the library.

"I am?" As far as I could remember, last time she saw me I'd had a slight cold.

I had a horrible feeling she was going to hug me.

She was.

One or two people turned round. Ursula coughed and asked us if we could keep our voices down, but Brenda took no notice.

"One of these days," she went on. "I'm going to winkle out your secret and find out what it is that keeps you so young!"

"Well…" I put out my hand to steady myself on the counter.

I noticed that Brenda was carrying a rather striking red duffel bag with two blue and two white stripes around the base. She put it down on the counter. *Presumably it contained her… well, I don't know, whatever you need for flower arranging.*

"That's a nice bag," I whispered. "Is it new?"

"Oh yes, do look – isn't it lovely? They are selling them as a special offer at the market this week. Upstairs, by the pet stall." She went on inexorably. "How lucky that I ran into you, Charlotte. I was thinking about you only yesterday."

"Were you?" I said cautiously.

"Listen, I want to take you out in my car…"

"You do?"

"I've got much more time now I've retired, and I'm determined to be useful. I thought I could take you shopping, you know – or pick up one or two little things for you. And I want to drive you over to visit that sweet little old lady who lives by the park. She never gets out – it would be so nice if you two could have tea together, now wouldn't it?"

Ursula glanced pointedly at the clock above the door and Brenda realised she was going to be late for her flower arranging. She gave a gasp, gathered up her red duffel bag and departed.

"Thanks, Ursula!" I said, and I didn't just mean the book she'd hidden under the counter for me.

Ursula grinned and turned to the queue which had formed by now.

Oliver gave me a lift home from Meeting the following Sunday and stayed for some soup and a bite to eat. He hadn't seen Jenny's Great Wall postcard before.

"So, you've heard from your globe-trotting grand-daughter, have you? When's she coming back?"

"With luck, in time for my birthday! I'm so pleased."

I cut some bread and put it on the table between us.

"What's she going to do next, do you know?" he asked.

I sighed. "Well obviously not go back into her father's stationery firm! She'll be lucky if Walter can bring himself to speak to her when she gets back."

Oliver nodded sympathetically. "Young people have such a difficult time getting started these days, don't they? Clearly, I can't take early retirement myself, can I – with my three still struggling."

I laughed. "My dear Olly, you'd be bored to tears if you left the practice, you know that perfectly well."

"Oh, but I could always devote more time to 'doing good' like our friend Brenda, couldn't I?"

I shuddered.

After lunch he told me about a day the Elders had asked him to give a talk at.

"Have you heard about that, Charlotte? Ministry to the Dying, Gerry's calling it. He thinks it's time the different meetings pool their experience on this. Some of the smaller meetings have had a few unexpected deaths lately, of quite young people."

I couldn't help smiling. "Did you say *to* the dying?"

"Yes, it's supposed to be one of our duties. We're supposed to comfort people, though I can't imagine what use I would be…"

"You could keep Brenda off them for a start! No that's unkind," I went on. "She means so well. But surely Olly, you should look for ministry *from* the dying?"

He sat back on the sofa and glanced out of the window at the sunlit lawn. "Ah now that's an interesting thought, Charlotte." He turned and looked at me. "Would you have anything to say about that? Not that you're dying, of course – rarely have I seen such a rude picture of health – but all the same…"

"Yes quite – I take your point. When one's pushing ninety. I don't know, Olly – this is difficult – you see. It all depends who I'm talking to."

He raised one eyebrow at me, the way he does.

"Death doesn't bother me at all, myself," I went on. "Certainly not my own death. It's quite bad enough, coping with other people's deaths, isn't it?"

"That's true."

"Oliver, do you remember old Horace, years ago? He used to say death was like setting out on a journey over an ocean to a strange place – he didn't know at all what it would be like when he got there – but he knew the boat builder so he wasn't worried about the voyage. I've always felt Horace was right."

"Ah yes, I like that," Oliver said. "Like Tennyson's poem – do you know it? Crossing the Bar."

"But so many people I'm deeply attached to these days – well, take Ian, for instance. He's convinced that this life is all that there is. I'm not going to argue with him. It's probably the right view for him, and in any case I don't want to get involved in all that; I'm far too busy living, just at the minute!"

"Yes, quite."

"I don't want to start talking about death being just slipping into another room. You know, Canon Scott Holland? If I say that, Ian and Ursula will find it impossibly trite, and I don't want to put them off because I'm so fond of them."

When he got up to leave a little while later, I asked him what talk he'd been asked to give, himself, at this day they were having.

127

"Well Gerry wants me to say something about prayer. He's put me in the slot just before lunch, so I doubt if I'll get much attention! Which won't matter because I haven't got anything useful to say. What about you, Charlotte? You could give me some ideas. Seriously, will you have a think?"

I smiled. "Maybe. The trouble is, my ideas on prayer were formed when I was eleven, so you might find them a trifle unsophisticated!"

We parted, promising to meet at the Brahms concert the following Thursday.

"You know Ursula is coming," I said. "Why don't we ask Ian too? I'm sure no one would mind."

"Charlotte, my dear old friend, you wouldn't be indulging in a touch of match making with our Friends, would you?"

I believe I had the grace to blush at that point.

"You're a wicked old woman, Charlotte, do you know that?" He laughed, and just before he left he added, "By the way, I've been thinking about what you said the other day – about Olive coming to your birthday barbecue thingy. Do you know, I rather think she might."

That afternoon I decided to have a look through Arnold's old trunk in the spare room in case there was anything that would do for the display Ian and Marmalade were arranging. *Surely there was more here than photographs? Ah-ha, there it was!* A small, tattered scrap of paper, folded in four. It was a letter, nearly all of it printed – with short gaps for words to be filled-in in ink – the date, the addressee and so on. I took it into the living room and sat down. It had faded yellow in eighty years, but my brother Freddie's signature was there as clear as ever.

Freddie disappeared when I was ten. That is, no one at home ever spoke about him. Nor did anyone in my cousins' families, not anyone in the village at all. I wondered if he could be dead like Tom – but surely not – for it wasn't at all like when Tom was killed. Then everyone talked about Tom, even the Vicar in his sermon the following Sunday. The Vicar had gone on and on about Tom and how brave he was to lay down his life for his country, even though he must surely see that my mother couldn't stop the tears pouring down her cheeks. But with Freddie – nothing – a blank wall of silence. Months passed. I think it was well over a year.

One day in the summer of 1917 I went down to the river and climbed the old oak tree on the bank. You could hide in its branches. No one would see you if you were up there, and my brothers had used it for games when they were children. But this July day I sat in it alone. I was eleven years old. It was one of those blisteringly hot days that you sometimes get at harvest time. The smell of haymaking drifted across the river towards me, and over the brow of the hill I could hear the noise of all the villagers at work. Here by the river it was quiet and I sat there for a long time.

All of a sudden I had the powerful sense that I ought to be thinking about Freddie. I had no idea why – I had not heard his name as much as mentioned – I could not remotely guess where he was at that moment: in England or Flanders? In Africa or Australia? Or was he indeed quite nearby, on an army manoeuvre on Frensham Common like the ones we'd witnessed when I was very young? All I knew was that suddenly it was terribly important to hold him in my thoughts as if he was in the palm of my hand. Just Freddie.

I didn't tell anyone of course, but the feeling stayed with me for days, a fortnight or more. As I went about my daily business all that time – lessons at school, some interesting, most utterly boring – walking home with my friends, cook's best strawberry jam for tea with her scones hot from the oven; all that time, underneath the surface, my mind – my whole being – was concentrated on Freddie.

As I sat now in my little flat at St Peter's Close nearly eighty years later, I looked at the printed letter I had unearthed from the trunk. It was headed H. M. Prison, with the name W. Scrubs filled-in in handwriting, and the date May 1917 – my birthday, in fact. "Mother" was the word Freddie had written after the printed "Dear".

The typescript read "I am now in this Prison, and am in" – here Freddie had written "usual" – "health. If I behave well, I shall be allowed to write" (here the word "another" had been crossed out) "letter in about" (Freddie had put "eight weeks' time") "and to receive a reply, but no reply is allowed to this." In handwriting it said, *my sentence is 112 days.*" Freddie had signed it and entered his Register Number.

It was years before I found out why it had been so important to think about Freddie that particular week in the summer of 1917. He had of course been imprisoned ever since conscription had been introduced early in 1916, because he was convinced that it would be wrong for him to kill. He'd been moved round several different prisons, travelling by train, and that summer of 1917 found him sewing mailbags in Exeter Prison, where in fact he met Corder Catchpool, who was a decade older than him and the first Quaker Freddie had ever met. As he and Freddie went out for exercise every morning at six o'clock, the men would look up and get a glimpse of the foothills of Dartmoor beyond the prison walls. They were haymaking down in Devon just as they were in Hampshire, and he caught the smell just as I did myself when I climbed the oak tree by the river that morning.

Just at that time Freddie developed a sudden severe

toothache. It was so bad he couldn't open his mouth to speak, which was pretty awful if you were kept in a cell for fixed hours every day and only allowed to talk during what he called "ekker". Even more depressing for my brother was that he couldn't eat hot food any longer; he had to let it cool down before he could tackle it at all. The toothache raged so long that he had to request to see the prison dentist, and he had to have two teeth taken out. It was, he later told me, the lowest point of his entire three years in all the various prisons he served in.

I took the official Notice of Incarceration round to Marmalade's bed-sit that evening, along with a few other letters from Freddie, and also a piece of fine silk that Arnold had brought back from China.

Marmalade was very interested. "So, you knew nothing at all about your brother Freddie being in prison at the time, Charlotte?"

"Oh no – his name was never mentioned at home. He was an utter disgrace to the family, obviously – white feathers, conchies, all that. But my mother kept that Notice of Incarceration in a secret drawer in her bureau. We found it when she died, just after the war ended."

"So, she never saw Freddie again?"

"No, but my father lived on for another twenty years – he and Freddie were reconciled in the end – though father never really understood why Freddie became a Quaker."

I showed Marmalade the other letters from Freddie that I'd found. He had written to an old school-friend from prison, since mother refused to correspond with him at all. The man's widow gave the letters back when her husband died in the Spanish flu epidemic, and Freddie passed them on to me when I grew up. He said I was the person he really wanted to write to, but of course that was out of the question; our parents would never have allowed it.

As Marmalade began to read the letters, I took my coat off and wondered about removing my jumper; it really was very warm in the lad's room. Then I remembered Rupert; *ah that was it*, Rupert required a constant temperature of seventy degrees. And there he was – I spotted him curled up in a glass tank on the top of a chest of drawers. Marmalade had taken the lid off and heated up his room to match the tank. I rather hoped it wasn't time for Rupert's Evening Ekker, as they would have said in Dartmoor. There were several branches of wood in the tank, all much the same colour as Rupert. He was coiled in the back corner and he appeared to be asleep.

"This is amazing, Charlotte. Can I keep these letters for a few days? I'll take good care of them."

I assured him that he could. As I left him, I picked up my coat from the bed and noticed a familiar looking red duffel bag on the floor.

"Isn't this nice?" He saw me looking at the bag. "I've only just bought it for Rupert – he's really thrilled with it. It was on special offer at the market, just next to where I go for his food."

I enjoyed the Brahms concert at the Town Hall. The four of us went in Ian's car, which smelt delightfully of vanilla. Oliver wanted us to go for a pizza first, but they were surprisingly busy for a Thursday and Oliver insisted loudly that they give me a chair while we queued for a table, which was embarrassing. Then he had to speak quite forcefully to some poor waitress, explaining that we had already waited fifteen minutes and we did have concert tickets. Ursula hung back at that point, looking as though she rather hoped no one would think she was actually with Oliver. *Oh I do love Oliver sometimes!*

After the fastest cipolla pizza I've ever eaten, we finally got there.

As Olly knows, Brahms' First has always been one of my favourite pieces. There's a tremendous sense of all shall be well in the end. It reminds me of when Arnold came back from China; it was the first concert we ever went to as a family.

Arnold had been with the Friends Ambulance Unit in China for most of the war. He was one of the oldest – at thirty-five he was already a doctor in a busy general practice – with a wife and three children. We had talked about it at length when another war seemed inevitable in the late thirties, and we had agreed – I wanted it as much as he did – that he should go and serve.

I had no idea what it would mean – how could I? It was just one of those decisions that you make in the dark, in trust. As it turned out, we didn't see him for five years; the children hardly knew him, especially Margaret. When Margaret got whooping cough and nearly died in the winter of 1942, I would have given anything to have had Arnold back there with me, but somehow one shrugged one's shoulders and coped, like everyone else in the country.

When Arnold came back he was a different person. He was exhausted of course, and I noticed that he didn't want to talk about his experiences in China when other men we knew spoke of their war service in the armed forces. But Arnold was full of exciting talk about the United Nations and peace and reconciliation. Quakers asked him to represent them on this and that committee – to travel again – to Europe, to America. I tried to tell him about butter rationing and the V2 bombers; most especially I tried to get the children to talk to him, but it was hard. Then one evening we all went together to an impromptu performance of Brahms' First in one of the earliest halls to be restored after the bombing, and it all began to come together again. Not suddenly, not quickly; I knew it would be difficult, but at least I knew it would happen.

As I sat here listening to the same symphony some fifty years later, it still gave me the sense of threads coming together. This party they were arranging for me, bless them, in Ursula's beautiful garden. It had already been announced after Meeting a few times, and a lot of people had told me they were looking forward to the occasion. Ian said he'd cleaned his barbecue for it. Gerry had already driven vast quantities of his elderflower wine round to Ursula's kitchen. Everyone planned to bring food to share.

And what about Ian? I must find out if he was serious about getting a job in Oregon. How could I persuade Ursula to put a stop to that?

I closed my eyes again, and Brahms came to a triumphant finish.

The phone rang on the morning of my birthday.

"Just thought I'd like to talk to my favourite nonagenarian," said a familiar, deep voice. "Didn't get you out of bed, I hope?"

I laughed. "Oh Olly, I should have thought you'd have known – I wake up long before this!"

"Ah. Actually, there was something I was ringing about, Charlotte."

"Yes?"

"I woke up this morning with the sun streaming through the curtains and first I thought, it's Charlotte's birthday, hooray!"

"Thank you, dear."

"And then I thought I'd offer you a lift to Meeting, and it suddenly struck me that this would be a great time for Olive to go to Meeting for her first time. And on to your party afterwards of course – what do you think?"

"Oh yes, definitely," I said, putting my toast down by the phone. "Great idea. What are you going to wear?"

"Well, I think your suggestion the other day was a good

one – the yellow gingham you said, didn't you? Very spring-like."

"Marvellous."

"So can I pick you up, then?" I caught an almost imperceptible note of pleading in his voice.

I hesitated, then said that yes of course he could, and I'd be on the pavement at half past.

We rang off, and straight away I phoned Ursula. "Sorry to bother you so early, but would you mind not picking me up after all, Ursula?"

"Oh Charlotte, don't say you're ill?"

"No, no – never felt better – don't worry. It's just that… Well, Olive's decided to come to Meeting today. She's never been before, and I thought a bit of support might come in handy. You know how it is. So I'll go in Olive's car."

Being Ursula, she understood at once.

"I'll see you there, then. Everything's more or less ready this end. We've just been putting chairs out in the garden. Isn't it a beautiful day? We're so lucky!"

"What about the barbecue? Is Ian bringing it to Meeting in his car?"

"No, he brought it round last night. He's just assembling it in the garden as we speak."

That's taken the wind out of your sails, I told myself severely as we rang off. There you were, trying to match-make those two, when all the time they managed it perfectly well on their own.

The next person to ring was Margaret, sounding quite mellow for once. "Have you recovered from last night, mother?" The family had taken me to rather a special restaurant the night before.

No one had as much as mentioned Jenny. I could see one of my sons was poised to say something like "wasn't

135

she supposed to be coming home for your birthday" when my other son caught his eye and shook his head gently, so nothing was said.

On the phone I thanked Margaret profusely for the evening, and we finished the call.

Olive was early of course – I saw his car slide past my front window a good five minutes before he was due. Before she was due, I suppose I should say. I can't cope with these different pronouns; I just think of him as my friend Olly. Anyway, I was ready so I just grabbed my favourite cardigan by the hall table and went out to greet my old friend. It's got gigantic pockets, this cardigan, which come in very handy for hankies and you never know what else.

"Oh, very nice," I said as I got into the car. I kissed him lightly on the cheek. "The lipstick is just the right shade, and I've always liked you in lemon yellow."

"That's good," he said as he pulled into the traffic. "I wasn't sure…"

Brenda's cake was produced after Meeting with the tea and coffee, so that anyone who couldn't come to the party would still get some. She really had made the most tremendous effort; it was a huge, rich, fruit cake, beautifully iced, with a large Ninety on it and various other bits and pieces.

As for the sudden appearance of Olive – well, most people at Meeting must have assumed that since it was my birthday I had probably brought along a friend or relation. They were a little startled when Ian hugged my "visitor" and Ursula kissed her. I saw a puzzled look dawning on Brenda's face, so I diverted her by asking what dried fruit she had used for her wonderful cake.

Before too long, most people had sorted themselves out into various cars and headed off for Ursula's home. As I arrived, I remembered to ask Ian what had happened about the interview in Oregon.

"Oh, sorry Charlotte – I forgot I'd told you about that! I changed my mind. I'm going to do a part-time Masters here instead."

"Oh, I'm so glad! I would have missed you," I told him, and he seemed quite surprised.

Gerry was already pouring out glasses of his elderflower wine in the garden. He'd set up a trestle table over by the rhododendron bushes, which had indeed, as I'd hoped, flowered in time for the occasion. Gerry's wife Bel was helping him. I felt quite honoured that she'd come after so long an absence.

I heard a screech behind me. "Bel how fantastic!" Brenda was powering towards us with the wind in her sails.

I caught the hunted look on poor Bel's face and remembered that she hadn't wanted a fuss. "Brenda – so glad you are here…" I came out with, before I worked out what to say. "Er… There's a dreadful crisis in the kitchen! Can you possibly come with me at once and see what's going on?"

Brenda looked slightly startled, but she dropped her red duffel bag and meekly followed me into the house. Well not followed exactly – she was way ahead of me by the time we reached the kitchen.

She marched in. "Now what's the problem here? What can I do to help? You just let me get on with it!" she said to Ursula, who was uncovering great bowls of fruit salad. "Or would you rather I went to help Ian with the barbecue?"

"Oh no!" Ursula cried gallantly. "Ian's got all the children helping him – piling on sausages – that sort of thing. Best leave them to it… Much better if you help us in here."

By the middle of the afternoon, after a spectacularly

splendid lunch, I must admit I was beginning to wilt just a little. I went upstairs to the loo – well of course she had one downstairs – but I love going upstairs in people's houses. There was a lingering smell of vanilla on the top floor.

When I came down I put my cardigan on and went to sit in the shade under a tree next to Oliver – Olive – that is. He – she – looked a great deal more relaxed than she had first thing that morning and was telling entertaining stories. Most of the others were sitting around on the grass at our feet. Marmalade was lying flat on his back with his hands resting under his head, his eyes closed. He looked very peaceful. Clearly not missing Rupert this time – ah no. I spotted that he'd brought his red duffel bag.

Over on the patio in front of Ursula's sitting room was the display that Ian and Marmalade had prepared, which had been much admired by everyone: the red silk scarf which Arnold had brought me back from China, Freddie's Notice of Incarceration, and a splendid array of photographs spanning most of my ninety years.

A comfortable silence settled upon the assembled company.

Broken by Brenda: "Now then, Charlotte – we must hear from you!"

"What?"

"This is your day, after all. You must tell us what it feels like to be ninety!"

I suppressed the impulse to say it was uncannily like being eighty-nine.

"Come on, we're having this great occasion just for you. It's almost like having a funeral, isn't it?"

This remark didn't go down too well. Several people said they looked forward to seeing in the next millennium with me.

But Brenda was not to be deterred. "No but it is

important to think about funerals. You ought to decide what to have at your funeral, Charlotte. Did you know," she went on, sitting up on the grass and addressing the company at large. "Did you know that you can get biodegradable cardboard coffins nowadays and have yourself buried in woodland?"

"Come off it, Brenda," Ian interrupted her. "This isn't the time…"

"No but this is interesting," Brenda said. "I picked up a leaflet about it in the library last week – you must know about it, Ursula."

Ursula looked blank.

"I've got it with me now, if anyone wants to see." Brenda reached across and picked up the red duffel bag. "I brought it in case…"

There was a pregnant silence.

Then Brenda let out the most piercing scream I have ever heard, and leapt to her feet.

"What on earth…" someone shouted.

"Brenda, whatever's the matter?"

The poor woman dropped the red duffel bag and collapsed onto the grass. There was a flash of grey at the neck of the bag and suddenly a streak was seen disappearing into the nearest rhododendron bush.

"Rupert!" Marmalade howled. He jumped up and dashed off into the bush.

"Would somebody mind telling me what's going on?" Olive had vanished in an instant and it was clearly Oliver who stood up and took control. The yellow gingham dress was quite irrelevant.

"Yes I rather think I can explain," I said.

An hour or so later most people were feeling extremely hot and sweaty. Brenda was lying down on Ursula's bed. Ian was giving Marmalade a stiff whisky and telling him everything was going to be all right. Oliver was organising the search in the back garden.

No one seemed to expect too much of me; well, being ninety does have its advantages, I suppose. I wandered alone into the front garden and stood at the gate looking up and down the road, speculating idly on how far pythons can travel. Very young ones, that is, those that are only thirteen inches long and likely to pine for their owners.

Suddenly a taxi came swerving round the corner and drew up outside Ursula's house, its engine throbbing.

"Gran! There you are! I've been looking everywhere for you. Mum said..."

Jenny threw herself out of the taxi and flung her arms around me. "Happy birthday, Gran!"

"Oh darling, how wonderful!"

She smelt of stale aeroplanes and crumpled sleeplessness and airline soap, but she looked great: sunburnt, her hair longer and prettier – and I rather fancied she'd put on a little weight.

"Gran, can I ask you something?" Jenny said several minutes later, when she had paid off the taxi and put her luggage down in Ursula's front garden for the time being.

"What, love?"

"Look at the pocket of your cardigan! Why is there a rather small snake...?"

Celebration appears in *Kingfisher Blue*, 1996, under the title *I Shall Spend my Pension on Brandy*

About the Author

Leela Dutt is an outsider, brought up in Golders Green by an Indian father and a Danish mother. From grammar school she read history at Oxford and briefly became a teacher. Later she sold dress fabrics, wrote for a local paper and then set up and ran a database on housing research at Cardiff University before becoming a proof-reader and review writer for *The Big Issue Cymru*.

She took a computing degree, beginning when her oldest child went to university herself, and recently Leela has set up the website attfieldduttbooks.co.uk.

She's married to the philosopher Robin Attfield and lives in Cardiff. They are both Quakers, and have three children, seven grandchildren (of whom six survive) and one great-granddaughter. Years ago they took their young family to live for a year in Nigeria, a formative experience for them both. Since then, they have travelled widely over the world – cheerfully, most of the time, as George Fox would hope. Travel inspires much of Leela's fiction, particularly her novel *Only a Signal Shown,* in which the heroine travels to many places that Leela has visited, including her father's ancient home in Kolkata which has been in the Dutt family for three centuries.

For more information about Leela and her books see attfieldduttbooks.co.uk

Like to Read More Work Like This?

Then sign up to our mailing list and download our free collection of short stories, *Magnetism*. Sign up now to receive this free e-book and also to find out about all of our new publications and offers.

Sign up here:
   http://eepurl.com/gbpdVz

Please Leave a Review

Reviews are so important to writers. Please take the time to review this book. A couple of lines is fine.

Reviews help the book to become more visible to buyers. Retailers will promote books with multiple reviews.

This in turn helps us to sell more books... And then we can afford to publish more books like this one.

Leaving a review is very easy.
Go to https://smarturl.it/ffxxk3, scroll down the left-hand side of the Amazon page and click on the "Write a customer review" button.

Other Books by Leela Dutt

Mathison
Published by Attfield

Imagine a computer program so intelligent that it can write a novel. This is the powerful story of one family throughout the twentieth century, involving an Indian home in Calcutta before the First World War, a Jewish dentist in Nuremberg in the 1930s and an artificial intelligence research unit in a contemporary British university.

The story moves from Golders Green via South Wales to Los Angeles. A Quaker business meeting in Germany in 1936 is interwoven with a Quaker weekend gathering of the mid-1990s as two parallel storylines starting at either end of the century gradually converge.

"Thoroughly enjoyed reading Mathison. I found the characters so engaging that they became like old friends and family. The book's clever plot device of an Artificial Intelligence program, that may or may not have written the novel itself, was both intriguing and plausible to me." (*Amazon*)

Paperback: ISBN 978-0-952978-20-6

Available from Amazon, or order directly from the author at attfieldduttbooks.co.uk/shop

Only a Signal Shown
Published by FeedaRead.com

Only a Signal Shown is a long-distance love story set all over the world, from Copenhagen to Darjeeling, from Stellenbosch to Los Angeles, and places beyond, covering three decades. Eleanor falls in love with Alec at university and travels to Nigeria with him, but is forced to give him up because she has to discover what she is truly capable of. She finds success as an artist and publishes sketches of places and people, eventually winning a prestigious international travel award in Kolkata. Meanwhile Alec is married with a family and has embarked on a career in television. They run into each other every few years, and become lovers again. The climax comes when Eleanor is caught up in the South African invasion of Lesotho and runs into a road block when trying to escape.

"This is a lovely book that pulls you in and makes you care about the central characters. Thanks to the author for writing it and sharing it with us." (*Amazon*)

Paperback: ISBN 978-1-781766-97-2
eBook: ASIN B008OS22WE

Available from Amazon, or order directly from the author at
attfieldduttbooks.co.uk/shop

Kingfisher Blue
Published by Attfield

First published in 1996, this is an anthology of eight short stories
involving fictional contemporary Quakers. The stories are all
written in the first person and are told by a wide variety of men
and women, often outsiders, ranging in age from 22 to 90. They
are set in Canada and Wales, in England and Outer Space.

Kate Attfield's line drawings add enormous charm to this book.

Paperback: ISBN 978-0-952978-21-3

Available from Amazon, or order directly from the author at
attfieldduttbooks.co.uk/shop

Other Publications by Bridge House

Gatherings

by Mehreen Ahmed

A collection of character based stories, some with a strong element of stream-of-consciousness style.

This book contains twenty-five unthemed short stories. The narratives are picturesque, evocative, and entertaining. They will take the readers on a journey laced with slightly amoral leanings to the serious and in-depth observations of the human condition. With both tragic and comic endings, vices and virtues, entwined into the hearts of the stories, they are all about ordinary people with mundane aspirations, broken dreams, and success.

Gatherings is a single author collection from Bridge House Publishing. Mehreen Ahmed has a well-established voice and is an experienced literary writer.

Order from Amazon:

ISBN: 978-1-914199-02-8 (paperback)
978-1-914199-03-5 (ebook)

Mysterious Ways

by Jeff Laurents

Mimsie Fotheringey's attitude to men? "Use them then lose them" was her motto. A modern day Adam and Eve undergo a repellant physical change. Is Emily Mayhew's real motivation about buying a house, or are her wants and needs a little more complex to say the least? Homes Under the Hammer takes on a new twist as people attend a unique auction to delight in the gruesome fate of the former residents of the properties on offer.

Mysterious Ways is a single author collection from Bridge House Publishing. Jeff Laurents is an enthralling story-teller who invites us to look again at what we thought was normal.

Order from Amazon:

ISBN: 978-1-914199-04-2 (paperback)
978-1-914199-05-9 (ebook)

Wishful Thinking

by Derek Corbett

A collection of stories in which justice is not always done but leaves room for some wishful thinking.

Relationships break down and are sometimes saved by money. Snowdrops bring precious memories. Brothers in a religious order have to find a way through some difficult decisions.

Wishful Thinking is a single-author collection from Bridge House Publishing. Derek Corbett takes the reader gently by the hand and offers us the comfort of a good story well told.

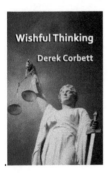

"An amazing collection of short stories, with a novella called *Glady's Time* thrown in too." (*Amazon*)

Order from Amazon:

ISBN: 978-1-907335-98-3 (paperback)
978-1-907335-99-0 (ebook)